Für Franziska, Matthias, Leonie und Julius
M.v.B

First published in Germany 2013 by Beltz & Gelberg
First published in the UK 2018 by Macmillan Children's Books
an imprint of Pan Macmillan
20 New Wharf Road, London N1 9RR
Associated companies throughout the world
www.panmacmillan.com

ISBN: 978-1-4472-5338-9

1 3 5 7 9 8 6 4 2

A CIP catalogue record for this book is available from the British Library.

Printed in China

Written by

Melanie von Bismarck

Translated by

David Henry Wilson

Flying Rabbits, Singing Squirrels

and Other Bedtime Stories

Illustrated by

Axel Scheffler

MACMILLAN CHILDREN'S BOOKS

Table of Contents

When Rabbits Could Fly

The wind was rattling the windows.

"What a gale!" Molly's father looked out at the back garden and shook his head. Molly was standing next to him. She pressed her nose flat against the glass. Her father shook his head again, and at that moment a gust of wind scattered the pile of leaves he had painstakingly swept up only a few hours ago.

"Just the sort of weather for a cup of tea," he sighed.

"When's Mummy coming home?" asked Molly.

"Soon," said Daddy. He went to the dining table

and picked up the teapot.

"When?"

"In two weeks' time, if you want the exact details. And now I'm going to eat her cake."

He helped himself to the piece of apple cake that Molly's mother had left when she'd gone to the station.

Molly sighed. She looked around the room and peeped under the sofa.

"Are you looking for Bertie?" asked Daddy.

She nodded. But the little cat wasn't there. Molly hunted for him in the hall, then in the kitchen, and eventually found him curled up on her bed. Holding the bundle of black fur in her arms, she wandered back into the living room and cuddled up next to her father on the sofa.

"How was school today?" he asked, putting one arm around her shoulders. With his other hand he reached for the newspaper.

“I almost flew away,” said Molly, “it was sooo windy!”

On the way to school she had struggled against the wind with her arms outstretched, and it had given her a mighty buffeting.

“So did you fly?” asked Daddy.

“Not really,” said Molly. “People can’t fly.”

“It wasn’t always like that,” said Daddy. He put his newspaper to one side and took a sip of tea.

"Once upon a time the sky was full of flying creatures." He put his head back and gazed at the ceiling. "People were up in the air meeting everything else that could fly: aeroplanes, witches on their broomsticks, dragons . . ."

"Birds, paper planes, basketballs, shuttlecocks, ping pong balls . . ." added Molly.

" . . . bouncy balls, beach balls, and so on," continued her father, putting his cup down.

"And flying saucers!" cried Molly.

"And . . ." said her father, patting Bertie on the nose, "rabbits. At weekends rabbits loved going for a flight with all the family behind them, one after another. The expression 'going for a walk' didn't even exist then. Instead everyone said they were 'going for a flight'. Donkeys, cows, horses, and even rhinoceroses could fly. But because rhinoceroses are so fat, they created

huge gusts of wind. So if a rhino just happened to fly overhead . . ." He took a deep breath, puffed out his cheeks and then blew out the air, " . . . you could find yourself caught up in a great big gust and be bowled right over."

Molly had a little think about this. When the wind had almost knocked her over this morning, might it have been because a rhino was passing by? But surely she would have seen a flying rhino. She tried to imagine what it would be like flying next to a rhino.

"Could everyone fly in those days?" she asked.

Her father nodded. "Of course. Everyone, even Aunt Elsie. Every day she flew off to do her shopping with a flock of butterflies. On the way she got them to tell her all sorts of interesting things about flowers. She learned that each flower makes its own sound, which only butterflies can hear. Their tiny ears pick up sounds like flutes from blue flowers, and trumpets from yellow ones, and violins from red ones. When a butterfly flutters from one flower to the next, he always hears a little tune. And on a warm summer's day, he and his friends can listen to a whole concert. Which unfortunately we humans can't hear . . . "

He broke off and fished for the postcard that lay on the living room table.

"In those days," he went on as he fiddled with the card, "Aunt Elsie used to fly over the Alps to Mallorca. A friendly eagle who happened to take the same route became her favourite travelling companion."

Molly knew why he'd just come up with that. The postcard was from Aunt Elsie. And it did actually say, in her spidery handwriting: *I'm flying over the Alps, heading for Mallorca.* But of course Aunt Elsie hadn't been flying alongside an eagle. She'd been sitting with lots of other passengers in an aeroplane!

"Flying without an aeroplane – how do you do that?" Molly wanted to know, gently stroking Bertie's little paws with her forefinger.

"You just need to do some regular training," Daddy replied without a moment's hesitation. Then he lifted his arms up, gave them a good stretch and waggled them around. "Good stomach muscles, strong shoulders – that's all you need. You only had to be a little bit sporty back then and you could fly."

Molly's father sometimes went swimming in the morning, and today he'd even been to a gym. Molly could see that he was feeling pleased with himself. She stood on the sofa, spread her arms wide and got ready to do a nosedive. Then she thought of something. "Did people have to wear helmets?"

"Strictly speaking, yes," said her father, stuffing the last bit of apple cake into his mouth. "U . . . o-o-y . . . o-e-e."

"I don't understand!" cried Molly, poking him in the ribs.

"But nobody bothered," her father repeated when he'd swallowed the cake and washed it down with a mouthful of tea. "That's why they always had air police on patrol. But all the same, every day there were flying creatures zooming through the air without a helmet, and bonk!" He hit his head against hers. "That could be really painful."

"So why can't people fly any more, but just birds and bees and things like that?" asked Molly.

Her father shrugged his shoulders. "Somebody fixed it that way." He thought about it. "Maybe . . . the world regulators. Yes, that's it – it was definitely the world regulators."

Molly had never heard of the world regulators. That didn't matter; she let her father carry on. He often made up funny things like that.

"This is what happened," Daddy continued. "While everything and everybody was crowding together up in the air, it was as if the earth was dying. Flying people filled the sky as they went to work, bashing against each other with their helmets. And if there were clouds up there and visibility was bad, then there was sheer chaos. Whereas down on the earth there was hardly anybody left. No one cared about what was going on down below, so it was all just left to itself. The machines in the factories stopped working, there was nobody in the houses, fields weren't being ploughed and lawns weren't being mown. In the end, there were plants and weeds covering all the paths, and they grew so high you couldn't move an inch."

Molly's father paused. She gave him a nudge. "And then?" she persisted. "What happened then? Why can't people fly any more?"

Her father breathed in, puffed out his cheeks, and then blew the air out again. "The world regulators got together to discuss what they should do. Wouldn't it be better if people stayed down on the earth? And while they were discussing it, they found a letter of complaint in their letterbox. It had been written by those people who had stayed on the earth and hadn't been able to go for their Sunday walk because the grass had grown so high. And this is what was in the letter:

Going for a flight is all very nice, but to tell the truth, dear world regulators, we would also like to go for a walk. Furthermore, a flying frog is a fine and beautiful thing, but we would also like to see a frog hop.

"And an ant run!" cried Molly. "And a worm wriggle!"

Her father, who was now looking out of the window, added: "What's more, I prefer birds that don't just spend all their time flying but that sometimes sit on a branch and sing."

"And I," said Molly, "prefer cats that don't fly around in the air but just lie there and sleep."

She yawned and stroked Bertie, who was still lying on her lap and very, very quietly purring.

"So there you are," said Daddy, also yawning, "that's why only birds and insects can fly today."

"And newspapers," cried Molly, grabbing the

newspaper and throwing it up in the air.

"Yes, of course, newspapers, I'd completely forgotten about them," muttered her father, rolling his eyes.

Molly picked Bertie up and put him down on her father's lap. "Now it's your turn to stroke him."

"Very sweet of you, thank you very much," said Daddy, but Bertie, who would rather have just carried on sleeping, didn't agree. He jumped down from the sofa and strutted away.

Molly kissed her father goodnight. Then she stretched out her arms and flew down the hall.

"Aren't you forgetting something?" her father called after her.

Molly came back, still with arms outstretched, quickly picked up the bits of newspaper from the floor, threw them on the table, flew down the hall again, and landed softly on her bed. Hardly had she gone to sleep when her journey continued. She flew over fields and forests, mountains and valleys, deserts and oceans. Then she felt a gentle breeze next to her. It was Bertie flying by her side.

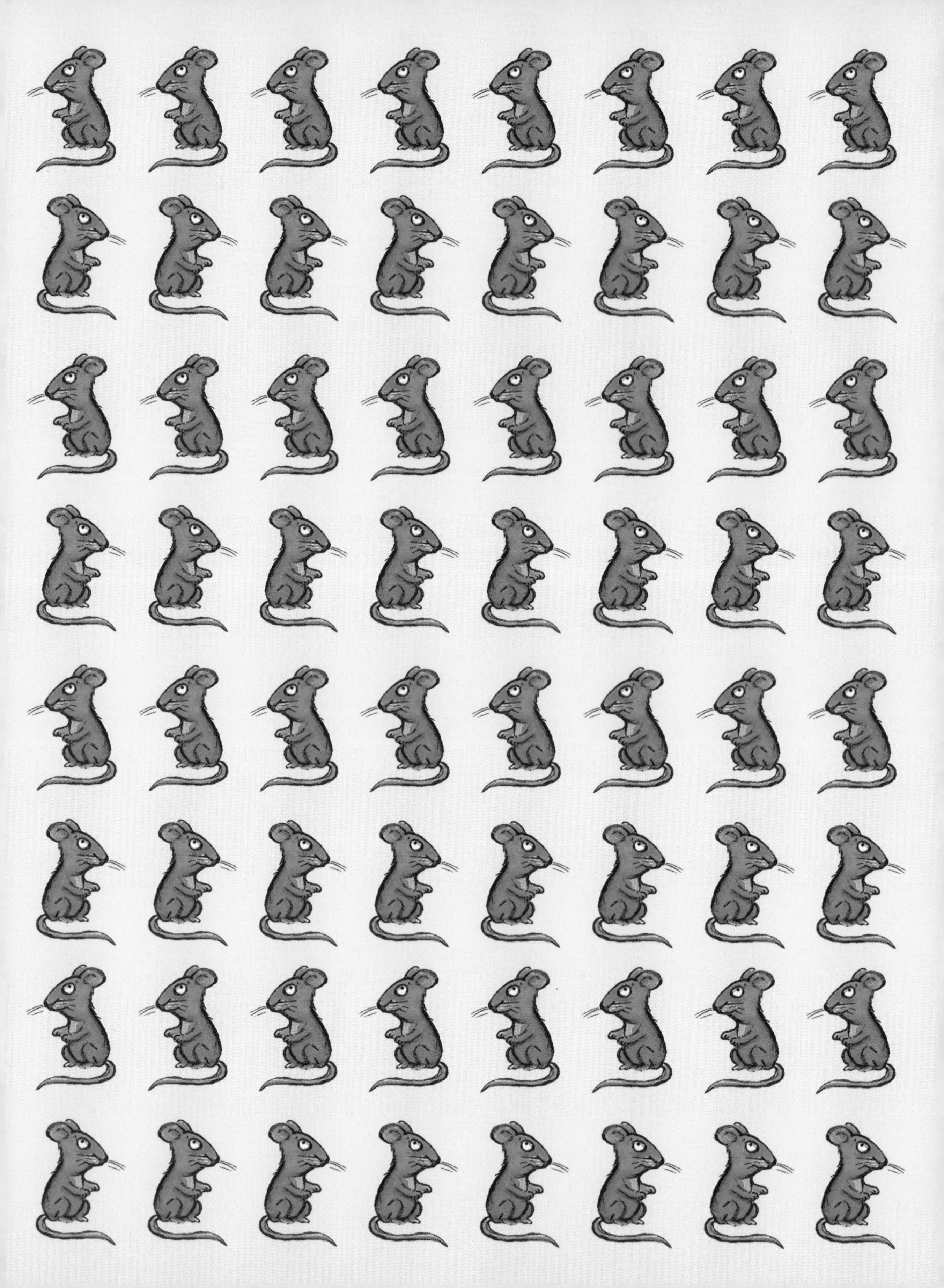

Green People

Molly was lying with her tummy on the floor, playing with her toy horse.

"How was school today?" asked her father.

"It was good," said Molly. "We were learning about different colours and looking at how many there are."

"It wasn't always like that," said her father. "Once upon a time, everything was green."

"Whaaat?" squealed Molly. "Green?"

Sometimes she thought Daddy was a bit mad.

He leaned back in his chair and began the story:

"There was a world regulation conference, and all the world regulators sat down together and made a decision. 'Things can't go on like this,' they said. 'Green's got to go. We need some different colours.' And why did they need different colours? I'll tell you. Everybody in the whole world was green. They didn't just have green skin, but they had green hair as well. And they looked for clothes that would suit them, so what colour do you think their clothes were?"

"Yellow," said Molly. Her father looked at her.

"I was joking, Daddy," said Molly. "Green of course – that's what you mean, isn't it?"

"Exactly, green," said her father. "People dressed very tastefully in different shades. But all green. Light green, dark green, lime green, leaf green. All other colours were out of fashion. Green people stood at a green table tennis table, knocking a green ping pong ball backwards and forwards. It was one mass of green. All you could see was green, and with all that green, lots of table tennis players simply went out of their minds."

"Wow!" said Molly, doing a shoulder stand on the floor. "Wow!"

"And when people went to the park on a Sunday afternoon," continued Daddy, "to play badminton and

have a barbecue, you could hardly even see them. The lawns, the leaves on the trees, the bushes – they were all green. It caused a lot of problems. When people walked towards one another, they often didn't realise anyone was there until it was too late. Then they'd start pushing and pulling and shoving and shouting. 'Why don't you look where you're going, you idiot?' someone would scream. 'Idiot yourself!' the other would scream back. You've never heard such a rumpus."

"I can imagine," laughed Molly, doing the splits.

"The insects," continued her father, "thought the people were part of the park, so they came and sat on them. So did the birds. The visitors to the park would walk around with birds on their heads. The birds found it nice and comfortable. So comfortable that they gradually forgot how to fly. Their wings wasted away, they got fatter and fatter, and in the end they couldn't fly at all."

"Oh dear!" murmured Molly, now trying to wrap one leg round her head.

"Even the food was green. Not just the peas, the beans and the salad. Other dishes were also coloured green. Imagine breakfast with green bread and green strawberry jam, and lunch with green spaghetti and green tomato sauce, and supper with green roast potatoes."

"Yuck!" Molly pulled a face and stuck out her tongue.

"Precisely," said Daddy. "Nobody liked that very much. In fact, quite the opposite. Nobody wanted to eat any more. Your Aunt Elsie couldn't even swallow a mouthful. She got thinner and thinner, and none of her dresses fitted her."

Molly did a somersault and tried to imagine how Aunt Elsie might have looked when she was so thin, but she found that difficult.

"People everywhere had lost their appetites. And so the world regulators got together to solve the problem. They decided to put an end to all the greenery. The first thing that was needed was lots of different colours for people. Next, pots and pots of paint were mixed together, all the houses were given new colours, dresses had patterns again, and there were bunches of flowers in red, yellow, blue, pink and orange."

"And bright things like my T-shirt!" cried Molly, and went hopping around the living room before hopping up onto her father's lap and giving him a goodnight kiss.

Of course she knew very well that her father's favourite colour was green. But it was great that he could make a bedtime story out of it!

When she was in bed, she gazed for a while at her bedclothes, which had golden moons on a blue background. Then she dreamed of green ice cream that tasted of vanilla.

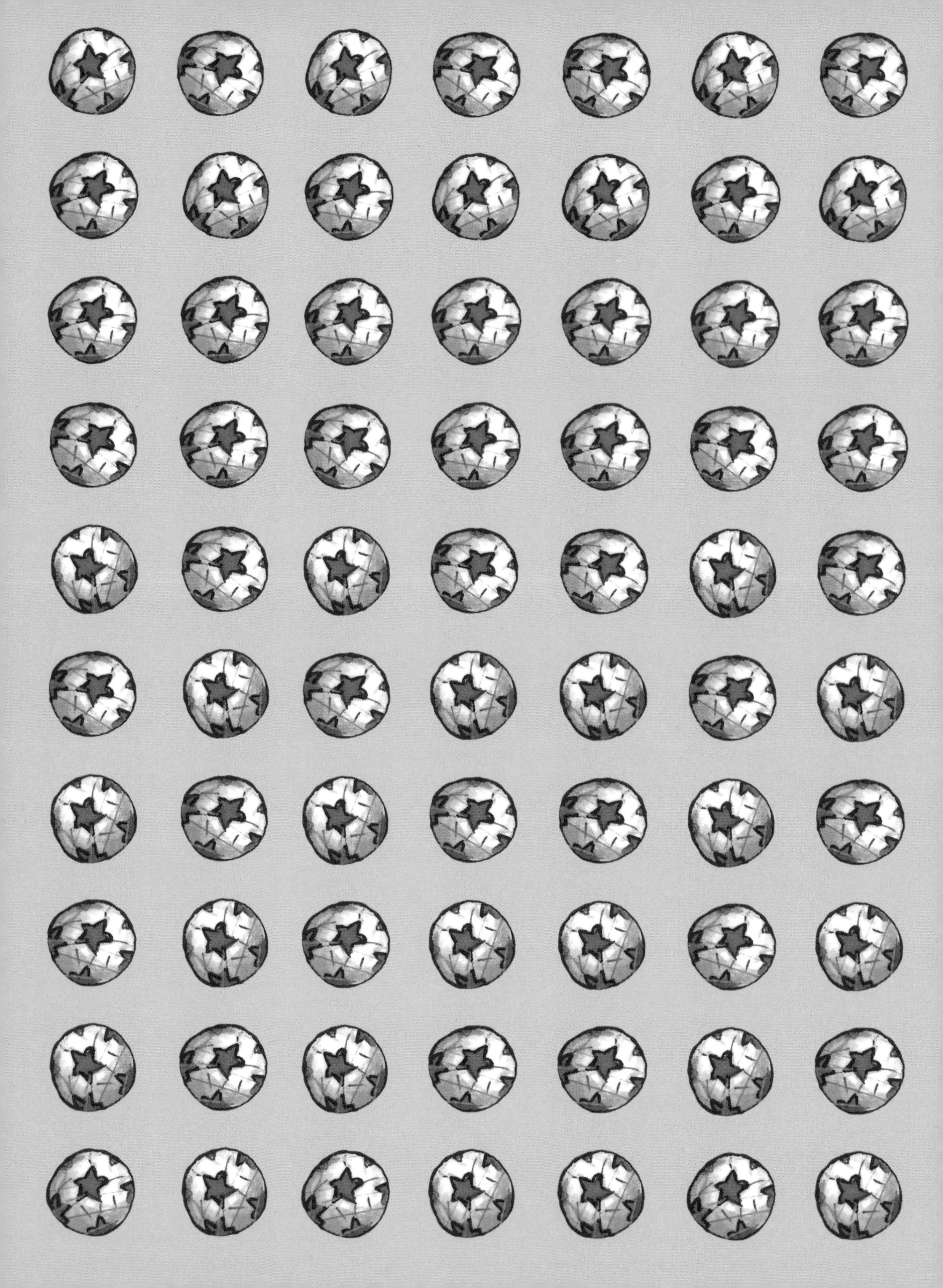

Why There is No More Time Travel

The wind whistled round the house. With one hand Molly pushed the door shut behind her, and with the other she held onto her ball. She had actually wanted to go and play football before supper, but the wind had whipped the rain into her face and the ball had flown all over the place – except where she wanted it to go.

She pulled off her wellies, threw her raincoat over them, and went into the kitchen. Daddy was making some cheese sandwiches. A mouth-watering pile was

already heaped up on a plate, and Molly helped herself.

"How was the museum?" asked her father, because Molly's class had been on a school trip that day.

"We saw at least ten thousand pictures," said Molly with her mouth full, "and we painted some ourselves." Molly hopped ahead of her father into the living room and he put the plate of cheese sandwiches down on the table. There were pictures on the wall here too, but nowhere near as many as in the museum. With her sandwich in her hand, Molly went from one picture to another.

"We looked at pictures from a long time ago," she said as she chewed. "When people used to wear really funny clothes, and there weren't any cars but just horse-drawn carriages." She sighed. "I wish I could live in a time when there were just horse-drawn carriages."

"Yes, well," said her father, "unfortunately it's not that easy to travel to another time. But it wasn't always like that."

Molly tried to say something, but instead of words it was breadcrumbs and bits of cheese that came out of her mouth.

"For example," began her father, "once upon a time you could go back to the age of the dinosaurs."

"Pooh!" said Molly, letting out another shower of breadcrumbs. "That only happens in films."

"If you say so," said Daddy huffily, and looked up at the ceiling. "In that case I shan't say another word."

Molly rolled her eyes, hopped over to the sofa and gave him an encouraging prod in the ribs.

"Go on."

Her father twirled and twiddled his cheese sandwich as he had a good think. Molly waited, grabbed hold of Bertie and squeezed him tightly against herself. The cat tried to get away, wriggled round and jumped off in a high arc. As he did so, his tail knocked the cheese sandwich out of Daddy's hand.

Daddy let out a groan. "Once upon a time," he said, picking his sandwich up off the floor, "cats were only cuddled when they wanted to be cuddled. Compulsory cat cuddling was strictly forbidden."

"That must have been a long time ago," said Molly, crossing her arms.

"It was in the year 1780 at the French court in the Palace of Versailles," said her father. "Anyone who went there could go and see Queen Marie Antoinette and her friends. Everything was pink. With their delicate little teacups in their delicate little hands, they would spend the whole day sitting bolt upright on their delicate little chairs. It would certainly have done them good to have a bit of your compulsory cuddling. But there was no sign of any cuddling. Quite the opposite: these fine ladies spent their time whispering nasty secrets in each other's ears, gossiping and talking about their hair. They wore white wigs which they piled up in incredible styles."

"I've seen them!" cried Molly, jumping up and down on the sofa so excitedly that her father had no choice but to bounce up and down with her. "In a picture in the museum! One woman actually had a

sailing boat on her head!"

Bertie glided past the sofa. Molly picked him up with both hands and put him on her head. This turned out to be not such a good idea.

"Look, Daddy, a catstyle!" cried Molly, but then Bertie sank his claws into her hair, slid down one side and finally clung by one paw to her ear.

"Ow!" screamed Molly.

"Miaow!" screeched Bertie, and he let go, fell down, jumped off the sofa and disappeared.

Molly rubbed her ear. Then she set about doing another compulsory cuddle, and this time her father was the victim. She wound both arms round him and hugged him as tightly as she could. Only when she spotted two blackbirds pecking for worms in the garden did she let go and run to the window.

She looked out for a little while. The wind and rain were stopping, and it was starting to get dark.

"Could people travel to the Stone Age, too?" she asked, turning to her father. She knew that he liked reading books about the time when there were tools made of stone.

He nodded and looked at the two blackbirds, which had just flown up into a tree with their supper. "Yes, of course. And in those days people still lived in trees."

"Why did they do that?" asked Molly in surprise.

"To protect themselves against hungry lions and bears," said Daddy. "And from up there they could spot other dangers much sooner – forest fires, thunderstorms, and of course stupid boys who were out to make trouble. They also had a much better view."

He brushed the crumbs off the sofa, stretched out and made himself comfortable. Then he went on with his tale.

"That was only possible because there were baobab trees then, growing all over the place. They were so

gigantic that at least twenty people could easily sit on them. Oh, what am I saying? Hundreds! The Stone Age children sat on branches where there was more space than in our living room. They played Stone Age ludo with counters made of stone. In the Paper Age, of course, the counters were made of paper."

"The Paper Age?" asked Molly, gazing at her father with her head on one side. He rustled his newspaper, which he had just picked up, and she knew why he'd suddenly thought of the Paper Age.

"You could travel to the Paper Age just as you could travel to the Stone Age," he said. "In those days, almost everything was made of paper: plates, cups, jumpers, dresses, jeans. Even the houses were built out of paper. Of course they weren't particularly solid. If children jumped around too much, the walls would start to buckle and bend, and sometimes a house would simply collapse. The houses had newspapers stuck all over them, too. The advantage of that was that wherever you looked there was always something to read. And if, for example, you were waiting for a bus at the bus stop, children could grab some newspaper off a house, scrunch it up into a ball and have a paper ball fight. In the end, the piles of paper balls would be so high that you could have great fun diving into them. And in the open-air swimming pool the children dived from the diving board into the pool, but instead of water it was full of soft paper balls."

Daddy took a little break. Molly tried to imagine what it would be like to swim in a sea of paper balls. Then she asked the question she'd been waiting to ask all this time. "How did people actually travel to the Stone Age and the Paper Age?"

"In a time machine," her father explained. "It looked like a small car. You got in, tapped out your destination and quick as a flash, there you were. Nowadays you sit at your computer and play games about knights, but in those days you simply got in your time machine, flew to the Middle Ages and took part in a real tournament. In your shining armour you'd have charged at the Black Knight and of course you'd have beaten him."

Daddy stretched his arms. "And as for me, I'd have spent the time bathing in the castle moat, after which I'd have attended a banquet with some beautiful courtly damsels, serenaded by a band of minstrels."

He stood up and looked at the pictures on the

living room wall as if he was in a museum. Molly waited expectantly to hear what he would come up with next.

"You could even fly back to meet the great artists at the time of the Renaissance," he continued. "Leonardo da Vinci, for example." Molly had never heard of him. "Your Aunt Elsie was one of Leonardo's greatest fans and used to visit him regularly in his studio. Once he was painting a portrait of a woman. Elsie thought it was wonderful. 'What a beautiful woman! What's her name?' she asked.

'I was thinking of Mona,' replied Leonardo. Aunt Elsie summoned up all her courage and asked Leonardo for a favour.

'You'd make me very happy,' she said, 'if you would call her Lisa instead of Mona. My real name, you see, is Elisabeth.'

Leonardo agreed. 'Yeah, OK,' he said, 'but I don't want to drop Mona. I'll give her both names: Lisa Mona.'

But Aunt Elsie still wasn't happy. 'Lisa Mona sounds funny. I think Mona Lisa is better.'

'Done!' cried Leonardo. 'So from now on she'll be called Mona Lisa.'

Aunt Elsie was over the moon. But as time went by, Leonardo became more and more grumpy and uncomfortable. Because Elsie wasn't his only guest. Art lovers from all over the world kept flying by in their time machines to watch him paint. They stood round his easel and kept giving him well-meaning advice: 'I'd put a bit more red here, Signor da Vinci, and a bit of blue would look much better there.'

In the end, it all got far too much for Leonardo. He didn't know what else to do except ask the world regulators to help him. They shrugged their shoulders.

'It's your own fault if these time tourists waste your time, Signor da Vinci. You're the one who invented time travel!'"

Molly frowned, but she didn't say a word because she didn't want to interrupt her father.

"Because you see, Leonardo wasn't just a painter; he was an engineer and an inventor as well. He built war machines and flying machines, and while he was at it, he also built a time machine. But nobody knows that now."

"Oh yes?" said Molly with a knowing look. "Nobody except you."

Her father pretended not to hear, and went on: "The world regulators suggested to Leonardo that he should destroy all his designs for time machines. 'No designs, no time machines – it's as simple as that.' With a heavy heart, Leonardo agreed. The very next day, he burned all his beautiful drawings of time machines. And since then, there's been no more time travel."

Daddy had stopped to look at a picture of a blue sea under a blue sky.

"Did Leonardo da Vinci paint that picture?" asked Molly sleepily.

"No, Mummy did," said Daddy. "And of course it's a thousand times better than anything Leonardo painted."

"I think it's a pity there aren't any more time machines," yawned Molly. "I'd love to travel into the future and see how things look in a thousand years."

Her father shook his head. “No problem – you don’t need a machine to travel through time. Just lie in bed, close your eyes, go to sleep, and the journey will begin.”

Molly looked at the empty plate. She had eaten all the cheese sandwiches. She would have liked to take one to bed with her as food for her dream journey. Because she really did want to fly far into the future. She put her hand on her tummy and felt reassured: at the moment she was so full that she wouldn’t get hungry even on a trip through a thousand years. And what about Bertie? He’d just have to catch a few mice. Because obviously her cat would have to go with her.

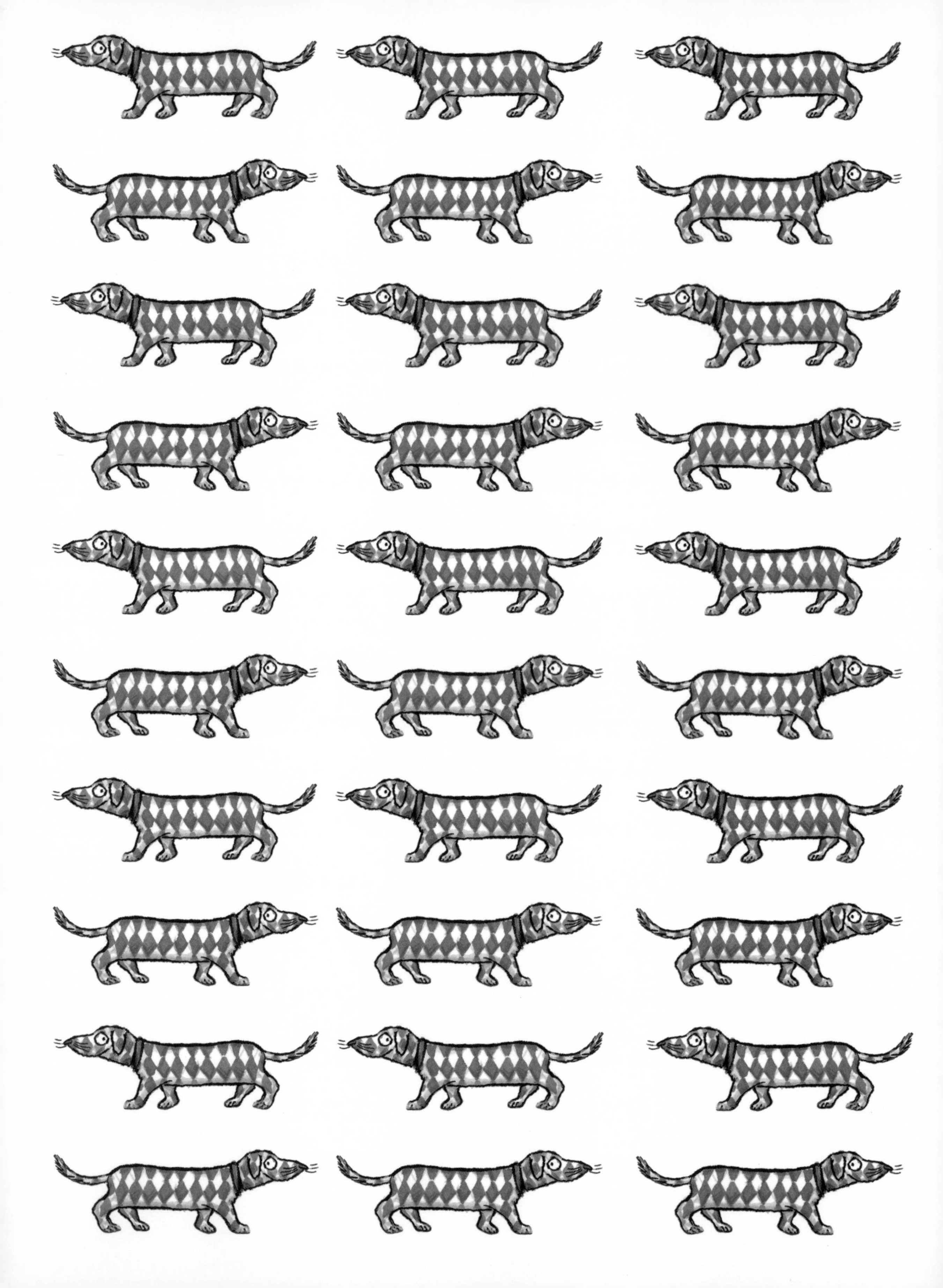

The Blue and White Check Friendship Sausage Dog

Molly's father swung open the door to the living room. "Phew, that was a long day!" he sighed as he threw his briefcase onto the table. Then he saw his daughter, and stood rooted to the spot.

Molly was sitting on the sofa, a picture of misery. Her eyes were full of tears and her shoulders drooped. "They're all so stupid!" she cried.

Daddy put his arms around her. "You're right," he said. "They're all stupid. Without exception – all totally stupid!" Then after a while he asked, "Has the donkey got a name?"

"What donkey?" Molly looked up.

"The donkey that gave you a kick in the teeth."

Molly looked down at the floor again. "Duncan," she said. "I think his name's Duncan."

Her father nodded. "Duncan the donkey, that fits."

Molly snivelled. "I've been at my new school for two whole weeks. And I still haven't got any friends. Only Henry. And now we've just moved here, Henry's going away. It's not fair!"

"Poor little you," said Daddy sympathetically, "not having any friends is tough, but it won't be that way forever. Hanky?" He gave her one of his huge cotton handkerchiefs. Instead of blowing her nose, she leaned her head back and spread the hanky out over her face. It was light and soft.

"Well now," her father began, "first of all you've got Bertie. Then there's Duncan the donkey."

"They don't count!" cried Molly through the handkerchief, which did a little dance on her face as she spoke.

Her father sighed. "Did you hear that? You don't count!" he said to the cat, who had just strolled into the living room.

Molly could hear Bertie stopping in front of her for a moment and then padding away again. He understood exactly what I said, she thought to herself, and now he's offended. She felt like bursting into tears again, but then she decided it would be better to hear what her father wanted to tell her.

"Now if the world regulators had any say in this situation, I don't think they would allow you to be so sad," he said. "They would do what they have always done under such circumstances. They would send you a blue and white check friendship sausage dog."

"What?" gasped Molly, and almost swallowed the

handkerchief as she breathed in. "A blue and white check friendship sausage dog?"

"Of course," said Daddy, in a rather superior way. "Don't tell me you've never heard of blue and white check friendship sausage dogs! Every child knows about them. I suppose I could ask if the world regulators still have one they could offer you – assuming the world regulators still exist and haven't retired yet."

Molly pulled the handkerchief off her face. She had

seen blue and white check tablecloths. And she had even seen a sausage dog in the park. But it wasn't check. And it certainly wasn't blue and white.

"A friendship sausage dog is a very special friend. He stays by your side all day long," said Daddy. "For example, he'll help you with your school work, because a blue and white check sausage dog is much cleverer than your normal sausage dog. He knows a whole lot of card tricks. And when he barks, he drives all your sad thoughts away. His nose is so sensitive that he can smell his way home and rescue you if you get lost because you've been playing with your friends and have gone too deep into the woods."

"But I haven't got any friends!" moaned Molly. Then she folded her arms across her chest and said sulkily, "I don't want a friendship sausage dog."

"No problem," replied her father cheerfully. "I remember now, the world regulators have got lots of other animals they can send to sad children. The tap-dancing elephant, for example."

Daddy stood up, stretched out his arms, and delicately placed one foot on the floor, first on tiptoe, then on his heel, and then on each in turn. Next he hopped from one foot to the other, did it again, and finally began to dance faster and faster, at the same time waggling his legs in all directions.

"The tap-dancing elephant," he said, prancing and dancing, and very soon puffing and panting, "wore black polished shoes with metal plates attached to the soles. Clickety-click, clackety-clack." He spun round in a circle with a clickety-click and a clackety-clack, and

slapped his thighs with his hands.

"And because the tap-dancing elephant has four legs," panted Daddy, "he can perform incredibly difficult and complicated dances that no human could ever do!"

He collapsed, exhausted, into his chair.

Molly wanted to try it herself. But after just a few

steps she lost interest, and sat all hunched up on the sofa again. There simply wasn't any way she could be cheered up.

"I don't think the tap-dancing elephant and Duncan the donkey would get on," she grumbled grumpily, "and I think the elephant would hide because he'd be afraid the donkey would bite his ear off."

"Ah, I didn't think of that," sighed her father, who was still a bit out of breath. "Right then, no friendship sausage dog and no tap-dancing elephant." He stood up, went out, and came back with a little bag full of frog-shaped sweets.

"I've still got a few enchanted princes in reserve, especially for girls who are in a particularly bad mood. Here, kiss the frog and he'll turn into a prince."

Daddy held the bag out towards Molly. She dipped in and managed to pick out a frog that had no legs and didn't even look like a frog.

"He's a little bit out of shape," said Daddy. "I don't think he'll turn into a prince, or if he does, then he'll be a rather unprincely one."

But instead of kissing him, Molly stuffed the frog into her mouth and noisily gobbled him up.

"Right, so not even an unprincely prince," said Daddy.

There they sat, Molly and her father. They looked out of the window. It was dark outside.

"I wish Mummy would come home," said Molly after a while. "And I want a horse."

Her father put his head in his hands. "That's something new," he murmured.

"Do you know the brown horse with the white nose?" asked Molly, climbing onto his lap and poking his arm with her forefinger.

He nodded. "You mean the horse in the field behind the woods?"

"That's right," said Molly. "I really like it." She thought of its soft nostrils and the warm air it had blown into her face.

"It's a fat horse," she said thoughtfully.

"An incredibly fat horse," said Daddy.

"Maybe there's a little horse in the tummy of the fat horse," suggested Molly.

"Maybe," yawned Daddy, "but it's extremely unlikely, because the fat horse is a male horse. But with horses you never know from one day to the next. Tomorrow's Saturday, so if you like we'll go there in the morning and ask the horse itself."

Molly nodded. That was a good plan. Then she found herself yawning so hard that she was afraid she would never be able to close her mouth again.

"Tonight I'll carry you to bed. All aboard!" cried Daddy, and hoisted her onto his back.

"Giddy-up!" she cried as he galloped down the hall.

Molly let herself drop down onto the bed. Daddy tucked her in and turned the light off. What a useful thing, thought Molly, to have a horse that can tuck you in and turn the light off. She could feel something soft at her feet. It was Bertie, who had already gone to sleep. Molly tickled him a little with her toes, but then she went to sleep as well. In her dream, the fat horse with the white nose came to her bed. Molly said to the horse, "I'd like to ride all round the world one day."

"Of course," said the horse. "Climb on, and off we'll go."

A Fish Ballet for Aunt Elsie

Molly had had a bath. Now she was wearing her father's huge blue dressing gown and she had wrapped a white towel around her head.

"Ah, here comes my princess," said Daddy as Molly came through the door. "In blue festive dress. May I have the honour, your highness, of offering you the seat next to mine?" he asked, moving sideways along the sofa to make room for her.

Molly sat down beside him and tried to sit as upright

and as royally as possible. Bertie the cat jumped up on her lap.

"I can hold my breath underwater for ages," Molly announced with pride. "Definitely a whole minute."

"Wowee!" said her father in astonishment.

"But to stay underwater for a really long time," said Molly, "you have to be a fish."

"You're right," replied her father, "but it wasn't

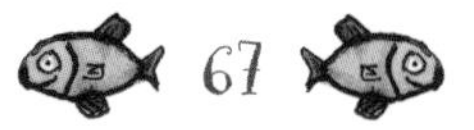

always like that. Once upon a time, people could live underwater, too."

"People?" said Molly. "So how did they get air?"

"Through their skin," said her father. "The skin could filter the water to get the oxygen that humans need. Exactly how it worked I can't tell you. They didn't breathe, and yet they still got enough air."

Molly looked at her father for quite some time. "Hmm, hmm," she said.

"People could live in the water or on land, whichever they liked," he continued. "You could simply step from the shore into the sea or into a lake, and go deeper and deeper until you disappeared below the surface of the water."

Molly remembered the lake in which she had swum that summer. She tried to picture herself simply walking further and further into it, until she finally became very light and floated in the water.

"Under the water," said Daddy, "there was of course a castle, and in the castle lived a princess."

"Was she as beautiful as me?" asked Molly, who had now stood up and with Bertie in her arms slowly waded around as if she was moving through water.

"She was fabulously beautiful, but not half as beautiful as you, your highness," said Daddy, also getting up and then bowing to her. "Every morning in the enchanted castle gardens, where the most gorgeous water plants blossomed, the princess and her friends would play underwater tennis."

"But a ball can't move underwater," objected Molly.

"You don't play underwater tennis with rackets and balls," her father explained, "but with reeds and seahorses. You have to hit the seahorse with the reed. And that's not easy, because seahorses are quick. You only need to give them the tiniest tap and straight away they're off in the opposite direction. But sometimes they swim somewhere else entirely. Seahorses have a will of their own."

That sounded great. Molly would have liked to play underwater tennis.

"Sometimes," continued her father, "they used to stage a fish ballet in the castle gardens. Aunt Elsie organized that. In those days she spent so much time underwater that she grew little webs between her fingers and algae in her hair."

Molly frowned. Aunt Elsie's hair was always neat and tidy. She would certainly have been horrified even at the thought of algae in her hair.

"Aunt Elsie was always accompanied by very large shoals of colourful fish: long ones, round ones, prickly ones, harmless ones, and sometimes even dangerous ones. Most of them obeyed her. She just had to signal to them with her webbed fingers, and straight away they'd come and swim in circles around her, one after another, scattering and then coming back together again. A fat and shiny puffer fish would do a solo dance. It was only tiny cheeky fish that caused her any problems. Great swarms of them would dash through her algae hair, and sometimes they would get all tangled up. Then of course they'd start pulling her hair, and she'd wave her arms around and pull her own hair.

The other fish would get confused, and it would all get chaotic. And that would be the end of the fish ballet."

Molly danced around in a circle with Bertie in her arms, but almost tripped up on the long dressing gown. Bertie was now feeling seasick and rolled his eyes.

"Could people play with sea creatures as well?" asked Molly.

"With some, yes," said her father. "The best ones

were the dolphins. Children would sit on the backs of the dolphins and be given a ride through the water."

Molly stopped dancing. She had seen something like that in photos: children stroking dolphins and playing with them in the water. She had often wished she could stroke a dolphin's smooth skin.

"Some people actually felt more at home underwater than on land," said her father. "They simply enjoyed the peace and quiet around them. These people used to live in houses on the seabed, and in the morning they would swim ashore to go to school or work. I think that's probably what my own ancestors did. I always like to go for a swim before I go to work. I must have inherited the habit from them."

Molly giggled. She knew exactly why Daddy went swimming in the morning – to stop his tummy from getting bigger and bigger. And swimming was certainly not an old habit of his. He had started doing it only a few weeks ago.

"If people went out of the water and onto the land in the morning, they would have been soaking wet," she said. She had taken the towel off and shook her head from side to side to dry her hair.

"That was exactly their problem," said Daddy. "Of

course there were beach huts all over the place with towels and wardrobes and dry clothes. But lots of children used to wander off to school and they simply forgot to change. So they'd arrive at school in dripping wet clothes. 'You'll all catch your death of cold,' the teacher used to grumble. But the children didn't listen. The school got emptier and emptier, because so many of the children were lying at home in bed coughing and sneezing.

And the teacher got so worried, she went to see the world regulators. 'This can't go on,' they all agreed. 'Living in the water and living on the land all at the same time is making people ill. We need to make a decision – is it to be water or is it to be land?' Then they had a vote. Almost all the world regulators were in favour of the land. And that was for one very simple reason – because the beds on land were a lot cosier."

Daddy stopped talking, and Molly suddenly realized how sleepy she was. She yawned.

"Time for bed, princess," said Daddy.

Molly stood up and stretched out her arms. She pretended to swim across the living room past her father, stopping only to bend down quickly and kiss him goodnight, and then she swam out in the direction of her bed.

It's a good thing, she thought to herself later, just before she fell asleep, that the world regulators voted for the land and not the water. I could never have taken Bertie underwater with me. He'd always have had to wait for me on the shore. Because Molly knew very well, after having tried once to have a bath with Bertie, that he couldn't stand being in the water.

Molly buried her nose in Bertie's soft fur, fell asleep, and dreamed of Aunt Elsie's algae hair and a shiny dolphin on whose back she shot through the water like an arrow through the air.

When the Whole World Slid

Molly had made herself comfortable on the armchair. She lay on her back with her legs up the back of the chair and waggled her feet.

"How was school today?" asked Daddy.

"I learned that you can walk all around the earth without falling off it." Molly leaned her head back so that she could see her father, who was sitting on the sofa and looked a bit strange from such a funny angle.

"It wasn't always like that," he said. "Once upon a time you could very easily fall off the earth. Or rather, slide off it. Because it was only at the last world regulation conference that they decided to increase Earth's gravity so they could stop people sliding off it."

"Tell me about it!" cried Molly, but first her father had to get his strength up by fetching a can of beer from the fridge. Then he put his feet on the coffee table and began the story.

"Earth's gravity keeps people firmly on the ground so that they can't float away. But in those days, its power was far too weak. And so everything on Earth was much lighter than it is today. What's more, gravity hadn't been properly adjusted. That meant that everything kept slipping a bit in the direction of the equator. People in the north slipped towards the south, and people in the south slipped towards the north. From the equator you could abseil down a hanging ladder to get to the other half of the world, to Africa for instance. You'd give it a good swing and then the Africans would grab hold of you

so you didn't go swinging off into outer space. And of course it worked the other way round as well. 'I'll take the hanging ladder,' people used to say when they were in a hurry to get from one half of the world to the other. That was simply the quickest way."

It must have been fun, Molly thought to herself. She could imagine herself swinging to and fro in space on a hanging ladder, back and forth, higher and higher. Right up into the middle of nowhere, among all the stars and without any solid ground beneath her. But then she had second thoughts. "Supposing you accidentally fell off the ladder?"

"Then you'd float forever all alone in the vast darkness of the universe," said her father, "like in an endless sea that you can swim in for hundreds of years without

ever reaching the shore."

A cold shudder went down Molly's back. That was no fun at all. You'd have to be really brave to go on a hanging ladder journey like that. "I'll bet Aunt Elsie would never have dared to do it," she said.

"Never," agreed her father. "Elsie's even scared of going anywhere by boat." Then he continued. "It was a very dangerous time. People were always slipping a bit towards the equator, and more and more of them fell right over the edge into outer space. Whole villages slid off. Very gradually, so you'd hardly notice. Then suddenly, oops, they were floating around weightless in space. Even now nobody knows what happened to the slider-off-ers. Some people say they set up a colony on another planet. And they're a lot happier there than they were on Earth, because the new planet is like a land of milk and honey, and whatever you need simply grows on trees. But nobody can prove it."

"Well I don't believe it," said Molly through a mouthful of the banana she'd just bitten off. "If people were sliding, why didn't they just grab hold of something to stop themselves?"

"They did!" said Daddy. "As a safety measure, the government had put handles and rails all over every town – on park benches, streetlights, trees and public buildings. And so people used to move from one handrail to another. It could even be fun. Especially for children. Without the force of gravity, they could jump incredibly high. All they had to do was give themselves a good shove-off, and it was almost like flying. Some children could jump so high that they didn't get back to Earth till half an hour later. It didn't take them long to get to school, because they simply jumped over the houses that were in their way."

Molly thought about this. "My route to school would have been super-short," she said, "but then I wouldn't

have been able to buy any sweets on the way. And I wouldn't have been able to look at all the baby calves in the fields."

Daddy hadn't finished yet. "But when the rhinoceroses and the monkeys in the zoo had all slipped off, and even the Mayor had disappeared into the Great Beyond, the world regulators called a conference. They were unanimous. This could not go on. All the clever scientists got together. Their heads were just buzzing with all the brilliant ideas they kept coming up with."

Daddy broke off for a moment. Molly waited patiently and folded the banana skin so that it looked like a flower. It seemed to her that Daddy was thinking very hard himself.

"In fact," he continued, "they thought so hard that smoke began to come out of their ears! And soon, the brains of the world regulators were smoking so much that the whole planet was just full of smoke. You could hardly see your nose in front of your face. The world regulators thought and thought, until at last one of them slapped himself on the forehead. They had completely forgotten the Big Wheel – the wheel that was used to adjust the earth's gravity. It had been such a long time since anyone had turned it. They needed the combined strength of a crowd of people to move it because it was

so rusty. And then, all of a sudden, everybody on Earth got stuck to the ground. They just lay there as flat as pancakes."

Molly let herself flop down from the chair to the floor. She stretched out her arms and legs and imagined herself being pulled downwards by an invisible force. She could not even lift her little finger. Bertie strolled up to her, leaned his head inquiringly over her face and sniffed. Molly lay motionless, still held fast by the invisible force. But when Bertie climbed onto her tummy and lay down for a catnap, it tickled.

"It looked really funny with all the pancake people stuck to the ground," said Daddy, "but it wasn't very practical.

And so the Big Wheel had to be turned back a bit. That's why we now have exactly the right degree of gravity, so that everything can stand pretty solidly in its place. All except for the washing machine when it starts

spinning. And except for you, because you can never keep still and are always jumping around in spite of the earth's gravitational pull. However, your bed, to which you will now be going, is certainly standing nice and firm."

Molly sat up and held Bertie in her arms. She looked sideways at her father, because she had just had an idea. "That story – you thought it up this morning, didn't you?" She had watched him clearing the wet leaves from the driveway with a rake, and had seen him suddenly slip dangerously on the slope.

"Yes, well," mumbled Daddy, "maybe, maybe not. Who knows?" Then he stood up and pushed Molly ahead of him to the bathroom, where she brushed her teeth.

Later, when he bent over her to give her a goodnight kiss, she grabbed hold of his jumper. "I need to hold on so that I don't slide away!" she said.

"But I'm a man, I'm not a handle!" protested her father, trying to break free. But Molly wouldn't let go.

"Molly, please!" Daddy was beginning to lose patience.

"First you must promise that you'll come with me if I slide into outer space," insisted Molly, "and that Mummy will come too."

"I promise," said Daddy.

Molly let go. Her bed was nice and warm. And it didn't slip. Then she dreamed that she was on a flying carpet with Bertie and her parents, floating through the starlit sky.

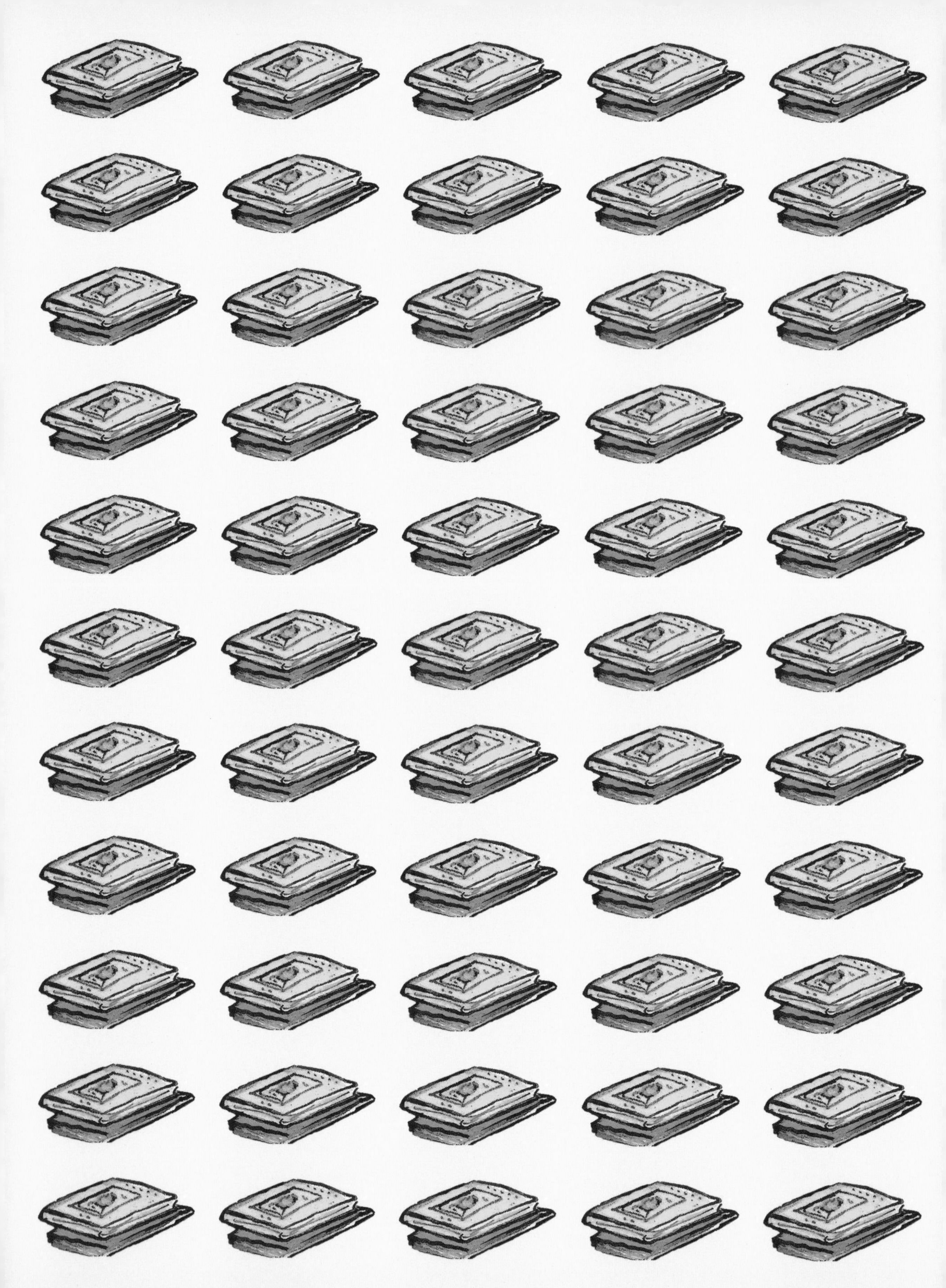

Molly Dances the Tiger Tango

Daddy very nearly tripped over Molly. Head resting on her hands, she lay sprawled out on the carpet reading a book and waggling her legs around.

"What are you reading?" asked Daddy.

"I've got to learn a poem off by heart for school," moaned Molly.

"So? I thought you enjoyed things like that," said Daddy, a little surprised.

"S'pose so," mumbled Molly. She pushed the book away, turned over onto her side and laid her head on

her arm. “But what’s the point of poems? Nobody ever speaks like that, with everything having to rhyme.”

Her father picked up his newspaper and poured himself a drink. “It wasn’t always like that,” he said, sitting down on the sofa. “Once upon a time people only spoke in rhyme.”

“Hmm,” said Molly. “So how did that work?”

“Very simply,” said Daddy. “Every child knew how to rhyme in those days. You can do it too. Think of something that rhymes with love.”

"Dove, above," Molly began. "Shove, glove . . ." Then she ran out of ideas.

"There you are," said Daddy, "you can do it."

Molly pulled a face. "Eeny, meeny, miny, moe, catch a tiger by the toe. I can do that." She shrugged her shoulders. "But if you just want to talk normally, how does it work?"

"I'll give you an example." Her father stood up, walked around the room, and stopped in front of the radio.

"'Will you turn that music down!'
Says Mrs Pepper with a frown.
'It's driving me quite up the wall,
I can't get any peace at all.
It seems to me you really oughter
Discipline your noisy daughter.'"

Daddy stood there triumphantly, hands on hips. "You see, it's easy!"

Molly pulled a face again. That was what had actually happened. Last week, a very angry neighbour had come to the door complaining that Molly was playing her music too loudly. She had been listening to her favourite song, and as sheep were her favourite animals – apart from cats, horses, squirrels, birds and dogs – she had listened to the song about a bleating sheep over and over again, all day long.

"Can you make up a poem about sheep?" she asked.

Daddy looked at the ceiling and bobbed up and down on his toes. Molly watched him. He was thinking so hard she could almost see thought bubbles coming out of his head. He took a deep breath, and then began:

"Baa baa black sheep's favourite food
Was rosy roses red.
The farmer, though, was very rude
And gave him jam instead.

He sighed and wished that someone kind
With loving words would greet him,
But no one was that way inclined,
And the farmer used to beat him.

Don't worry, there's a happy ending," said Daddy, as he saw the reproachful look in Molly's eyes. Then he went on:

"And then one frosty winter's day,
He said, 'This is no good.
I think I'd better run away
And live in Rosepetal Wood.'

In Rosepetal Wood what did he find?
A grey and lonely ewe,
Who said, 'I'm bored out of my mind.
Shall we be friends, me and you?'

So one grey ewe and one black ram
Are no longer feeling sad.
They've even had a little lamb
Who looks just like his dad."

That was the end of the poem and Daddy sat down again. "You see, you can tell a whole story in rhyme."

Molly decided that she would like to have a go, but she had to move around first to help her think. First she jumped up and down. Then she did a shoulder stand, and finally a handstand up against the wall. From her upside down position she now delivered her poem:

"Eeny meeny miny moe,
Catch a teacher by his toe.
If he hollers, let him go,
Eeny meeny miny moe."

She levered herself off the wall and landed feet first on the floor. "That's the only poem I can do."

"Ah well," said Daddy, "at least it rhymes. But it's not very original, is it? See if you can come up with something new."

Molly picked up her empty glass from the table. "Ninny nanny nunny non, all the apple juice is gone."

"Brilliant!" cried Daddy.

Molly charged into the kitchen and came back carefully holding the glass, which was now full. "I can do another nonsense poem! Easter bunny got no money, silly goose got no juice . . ." she sang, putting the glass down and dancing faster and faster in circles round the room. "Mickey Mouse in my house, eat my hat and Daddy's fat . . ."

"Whoa!" cried Daddy, as Molly went on, laughing herself silly. "Big fat belly, strawberry jelly, mixi maxi, call a taxi . . ." She collapsed onto the sofa. "Can't do any more. Your turn, Daddy."

"OK," he said. "But I need a word. Say any word you like."

"Mouse," said Molly.

"Ha, that's easy," scoffed Daddy.

"My cat saw a mouse on the mat
And thought, 'I'll make a meal of that.'
But the smart little mouse
Ran out of the house,
And made a right fool of the cat."

"Easy as pie!" said Molly. "Now I'll make it harder. Summer holidays."

Daddy was stumped. Molly slid off the sofa and

did a crab on the floor. "You see?" she cried, with her head upside down. "There are no rhymes for summer holidays."

Daddy flicked through his newspaper and shook his head. "Sometimes it's difficult to find rhymes. And in the end that was the reason why rhyming had to be abolished in everyday speech. This is what happened."

He put the newspaper down and crossed his legs as Molly did a cartwheel. "If you went shopping – this was in the days when everyone was still talking in rhyme – of course your shopping list had to rhyme as well. Some people found this too complicated. And so the supermarkets set up a special service just for them. Whoever wanted to could hand in his shopping list at the entrance and get a rhyming machine to do the rhyming for him. Sometimes the machine had to add an item or two to make sure everything rhymed. And for a while that was very successful. Until the day when Aunt Elsie handed in her shopping list for rhyming. When she got it back, this was what she found:

> Sugar, jam, potatoes, carrots,
> Thirteen packs of food for the parrots,
> Leg of lamb, milk of goat,
> Biscuits, butter, motorboat.

'Motorboat!?' screeched Aunt Elsie, and complained to the checkout assistant. 'I don't need a motorboat!'"

Molly giggled and did a few press-ups.

"'If I needed to buy a boat,' Aunt Elsie said to the checkout girl, 'I'd buy a sailing boat not a motorboat!'

'All gone,' said the girl. 'Sold out, I'm afraid. We've only got motorboats left.' Aunt Elsie wanted to get rid of the goat's milk, but that didn't work. 'Sold is sold,' said the cashier. 'Company policy.'"

"What happened next?" asked Molly, panting a little

because she'd just been trying to put both legs behind her head.

"Have a guess," said Daddy.

"I know," said Molly. "Aunt Elsie complained to the world regulators."

"Exactly. By now the world regulators had been flooded with letters of complaint because the shops kept selling out of everything that rhymed. Cake and steak, for example. Whereas anything that was hard to rhyme just got stuck on the shelves. Like cauliflower. That rhymes with jolly flower, but there's no such thing – it's just nonsense."

"Super-nonsense!" cried Molly, and immediately came up with a super-nonsense rhyme of her own. "Pickety pockety poo, it's best to wee in the loo." Then she tried to stand on tiptoe like a ballerina.

"There were rhyming problems at school too," continued Daddy. "The teacher kept having to say things she didn't want to say at all. For instance, if she was telling the children off, she'd say: 'All of you are lazy, and it's making me go crazy.' Then of course they'd all laugh at their crazy teacher. Or when she came into the classroom and wanted to see their homework, she'd have to say something like: 'Now then, show me what you've done, but if you can't, then have some fun.' So they'd laugh themselves silly, and rush out into the playground. And if they were doing a test, she'd say, 'Anyone who tries to cheat will have to sniff my smelly feet.'

Molly doubled up. "Bonkers conkers!" she laughed.

"Exactly," said her father. "And so the world regulators held a conference. And they decided to abolish rhyming from everyday speech. But it didn't quite work. Because there were a lot of people who didn't want rhyme to be banned. So they put up a sign:

For those of you who don't like rhyme,

The rhyming time has gone.
But those of us who think it's fun
Will simply carry on."

"You too, Daddy!" cried Molly. "Make up another poem about animals!"

Her father thought long and hard. "What sort of animals?"

"Any animals. So long as there are lots of them," replied Molly.

This time her father thought for at least an hour – or so it seemed to Molly. And then he had to go and get another drink from the fridge. By the time he'd finished thinking, she had tried pulling three new faces and done the splits as well as another handstand against the wall. But at last the poem began:

"There was a party at Molly's house.

With lots of animals there.
Including an African green mouse
And an Indian blue bear."

Daddy stood up, put his hands on his hips, and began a peculiar dance as he started to sing:

"Stamp and hop, leap and prance,
Do the tiger tango.
All the animals love to dance,
Just like Jackal Django.

Leopard, lion, panda, pig,

Monkey, mouse and mole
Join to do the jungle jig
And rhino rock and roll."

Molly jumped off the sofa, linked arms with Daddy and hummed the tune as they danced.

"Up on tiptoe, down at heel,
Slither like a mamba,
Fox trot, wolf-waltz, reindeer reel,
Stag stomp and snaky samba.

And if they're not asleep in bed,
The fat, thin, short and tall,
They'll still be dancing here instead,
Enjoying the animal ball."

And as Molly and her father were having so much

fun, they sang the first verse all over again:

"There was a party at Molly's house.
With lots of animals there.
Including an African green mouse
And an Indian blue bear."

Molly clapped her hands and would have liked to dance around for a bit longer, but her father was so exhausted that he flopped down into his armchair.

Molly sat on the window seat. Then she thought of another rhyme: "It won't be long before Mummy's here, and then we'll all stand up and cheer."

And Daddy replied, "Meanwhile, you've been entertained and fed, and I think it's time you went to bed."

"Oh!" said Molly, suddenly remembering something. "I still haven't learnt a poem for school tomorrow."

"Ah!" said Daddy. He stroked his stubble. "Well, instead, you and I made up a poem ourselves. In fact a proper song. So maybe you could sing that in class tomorrow."

Molly thought that was a good idea. If the teacher chose her tomorrow, she would recite the tiger tango and the mamba samba. She might even dance them as well.

When she went to her bedroom soon afterwards, Bertie was already asleep under the covers. Molly snuggled up close to him and felt his soft, warm fur against her tummy. Before she fell asleep, she tried to find a rhyme for Bertie. She searched and searched. It was only hours later in her dreams that a Bertie poem popped into her head:

> My little cat Bertie
> Loved a cat named Gertie.
> She didn't want to know 'im.
> That's the end of the poem.

The next morning, Molly knew that all the rhymes she had dreamed of during the night had been great. But unfortunately she couldn't remember any of them.

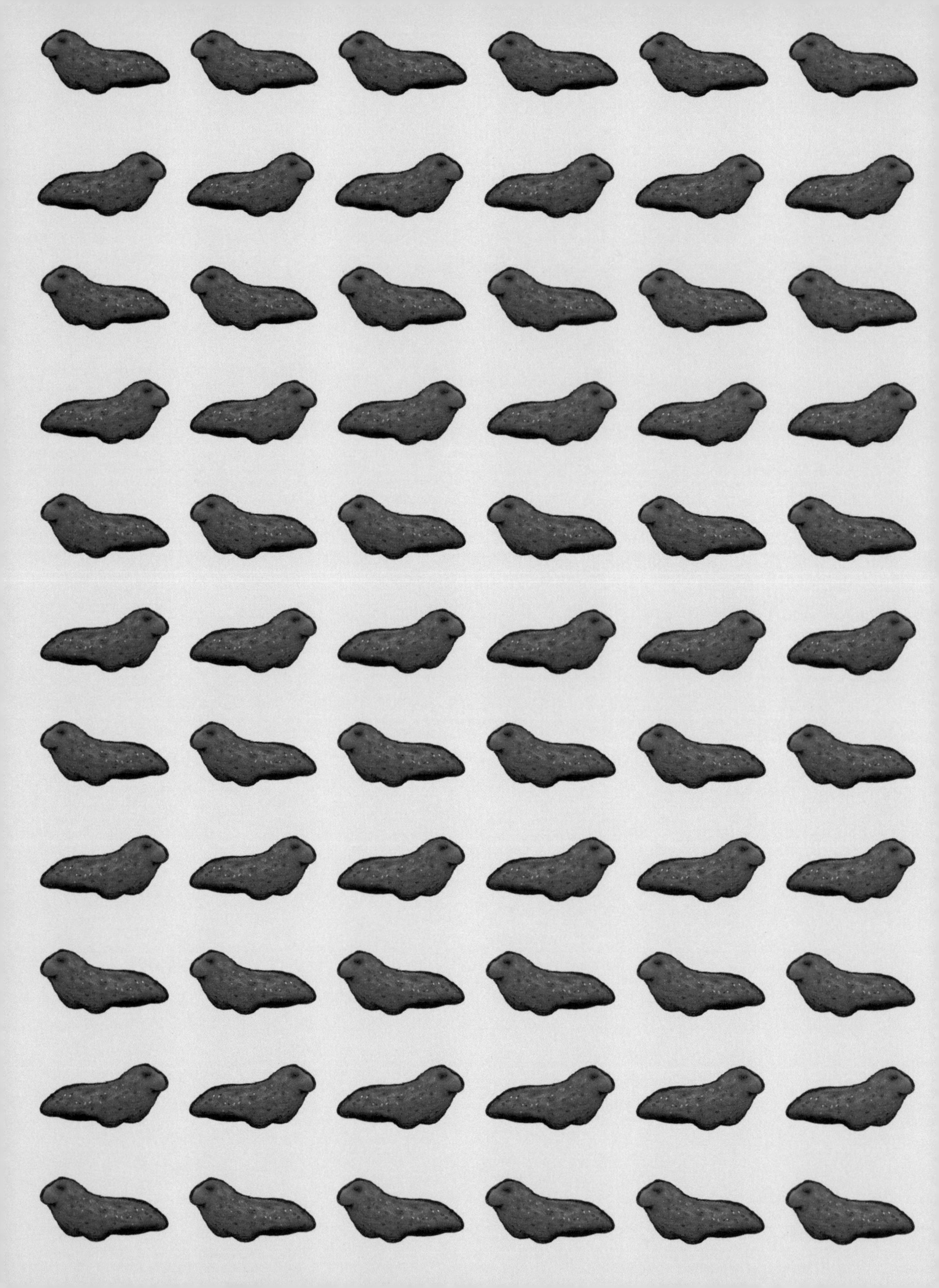

When Stones Were Still Alive

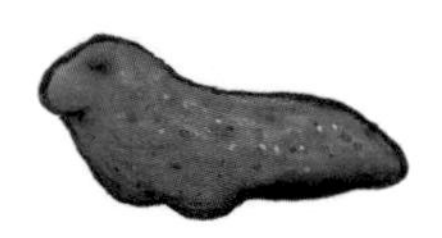

Molly was sitting next to Daddy on the sofa, wearing her pyjamas. She was holding a stone which she had found on the beach that summer. It was grey with white spots, had a soft smooth surface, and was a very strange shape.

"It looks like something alive," said Molly. "Like a seal." She held the stone out towards her father.

"You're right," he said. "It looks like a live animal."

"But stones aren't alive," said Molly, leaning down to stroke Bertie.

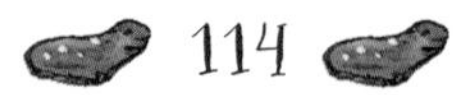

"It wasn't always like that," said her father. "Once upon a time everything was alive."

Molly shifted to the armchair. "A car is sort of alive, isn't it?" she said. "Because it moves. And an alarm clock. Because it rings."

"Well, yes," replied her father, "things like that work. If you're lucky. But that's not what I meant. Once upon a time, things were just as alive as people. They all had

a will of their own. Suppose you get into the car in the morning to go to work. The car says: 'I'd sooner go to the zoo today. You can come with me if you like. But if you insist on going to work, then please take the bus.'"

Molly laughed. If she had been a car, she would have said more or less the same. But she knew exactly what her father was thinking of: this morning, to his great annoyance, the car had refused to start and he had had to go to work by bus.

"In those days, when things were still alive, the nuisance started the moment you got dressed," said Daddy. He was now pacing around the room. "Say you wanted to put on your T-shirt. But the T-shirt didn't feel like it and ran away. By the time you'd finally caught it and put it on, you'd be so exhausted that all you really wanted to do was go back to bed. And that was just the beginning of the day! It carried on at breakfast time." Daddy was now in full flow.

"You couldn't get a moment's peace. You'd hardly poured out your tea when the cups would start jumping around, splish splosh, tea everywhere. Knives and forks danced in circles, and the pot of marmalade sang songs about the spring." Daddy spun round in a circle and sang: "Here we go gathering nuts in May . . ."

Molly giggled. She gazed at the stone in her hand. If it was alive, how would it move? Like a proper seal?

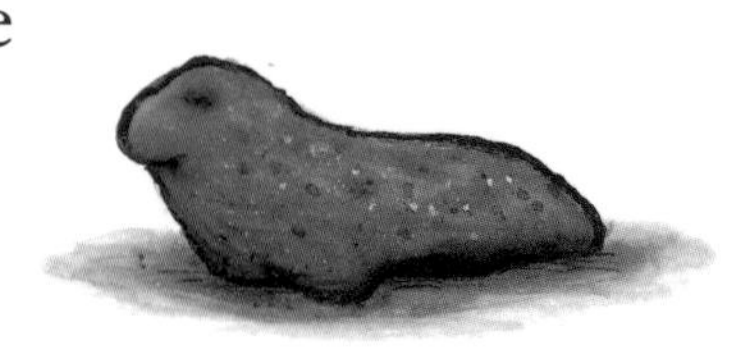

Daddy looked out into the back garden. "Things got more and more cheeky. They did whatever they liked. Apart from trees, which are very much alive even today. Trees were never cheeky, but always polite, always well-behaved. When you walked past them, they always smiled at you and waved their branches. And if they were in a particularly happy mood, they would even dance for you and bow."

Daddy bowed very low, and then grabbed his back. "Of course only if they didn't have a bad back." With a groan he straightened himself up.

Molly went and stood beside him. The way the branches outside were waving in the wind, they certainly did look as if they were dancing. Molly imagined herself walking to school through the forest early one morning and seeing the trees slowly waking up all around her and yawning as they stretched their branches up into the sky.

Then she caught sight of Bertie wandering around outside in the dark garden. "Poor Bertie!" she cried anxiously. "It's much too cold and windy for him. I must bring him in."

She opened the patio door, rushed out and seized hold of the cat. At that moment, a bush next to her lowered its branches as the wind whistled "wheeeee".

"Good evening," Molly replied automatically, and

she also did a bow. Then she ran back indoors.

"Out in the cold wearing your pyjamas and slippers – honestly, Molly . . ." grumbled her father, and quickly shut the door behind her so that only a tiny gust of wind could squeeze its way through the gap.

"So what did the living things do?" asked Molly, when she had put Bertie down and wrapped herself up in a thick woollen blanket.

"It became really dangerous for people when traffic lights started acting up," said Daddy. "You see, they were fed up with just being red, yellow and green. They preferred to be blue. Just for a change. 'What does blue mean?' all the drivers wondered when the traffic lights turned blue. 'Blue? Well, OK, I'll carry on – it'll be all right.' But it wasn't all right! Because all the cars suddenly drove off at the same time, and bang, crash, wallop, there was a huge pile-up at every junction."

Daddy rolled his eyes and sighed, "How can anyone be so utterly stupid as to drive through a blue traffic light!"

Molly knew how much it was still bugging her father that recently someone had dented his car. Although actually it had been his own fault.

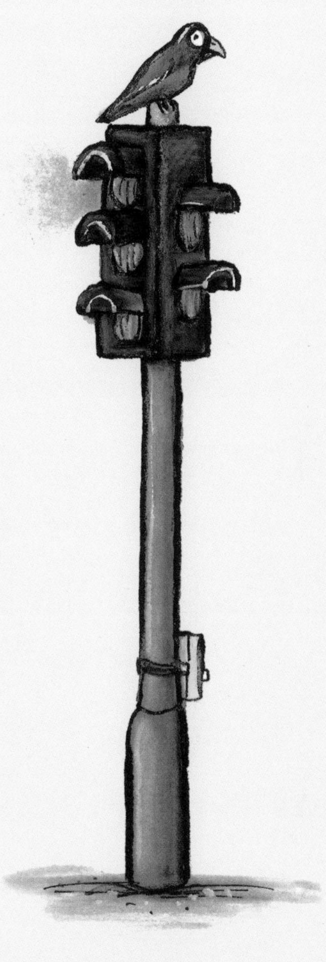

"And Aunt Elsie?" she asked, to try and take his mind off the accident.

"Aunt Elsie!" cried her father, flopping down into his chair. He thought about it for a moment and then continued: "Not a single watch or clock would work properly. Her wrist watch thought it was something special because it was made of gold. And so it thought it had to go faster than all the others. When the kitchen clock said three, the wrist watch decided, 'In that case, I'll say four.' Yah-boo to everyone else. Then the alarm clock got jealous and wanted to have its own time as well. So it simply stopped. And from then on, no matter what time of day it was, the dial showed seven hours, forty-six minutes and fifteen seconds. That meant that every Wednesday Aunt Elsie was late for her coffee morning. All over the world, clocks discovered that they had free will.

Alarm clocks woke people up when they felt like it – sometimes even in the middle of the night. Then children would drag themselves to school, worn out even before they'd started, and would immediately fall asleep over their exercise books. You can just picture it, can't you? 'Things can't go on like this,' said the world regulators.

'Absolutely everything will be all over the place if every little thing does as it pleases.' Nobody knows exactly how long they spent discussing the situation, because according to one clock it took an hour, and another one said a year. Anyway, in the end the world regulators saw to it that things could only do the work

they were supposed to do, had no free will of their own, and stopped giving humans the run-around. At least most of them did. Of course, that was . . ."

Molly's thoughts had wandered off in a completely different direction. She had now covered her whole body with the woollen blanket, and only her face was visible. "If my seal stone had a will of its own," she wondered, "would it prefer to eat fish like a seal or fly through the window like a stone?"

"The questions you ask!" groaned Daddy. He took the stone from her and held it up to his ear.

"Aha, mhm, aha, I see, very interesting," he murmured.

"What did it say?" asked Molly impatiently.

"It said that it's too late now for a seal stone to answer such a difficult question," yawned Daddy, "because for a seal stone it's now bedtime."

Daddy couldn't help sneezing, because Bertie had

just jumped onto the sofa and tickled Daddy's nose with his furry tail.

"Now take that ani . . . ani . . . atishoo! . . . take Bertie and then off you go to bed."

Molly gave her father a hug and a kiss and left the room. After a couple of steps down the hall, she came back again.

"Daddy, what does a seal do?" Daddy looked puzzled. "I mean, what noises does a seal make?"

"Something like this," said Daddy, and he did a sniffy, snuffly, grunty, growly bark. It sounded pretty awful, but Molly gave him another kiss all the same. Then she went to the bathroom.

That evening, the toothbrush went crazy. First of all it wanted to be a nailbrush, and then a hairbrush. After Molly had persuaded it to be neither, it decided it wanted to fly. The one thing it didn't want to do was go into Molly's mouth. The sponge thought it was all hilarious and wanted to copy the toothbrush. Then the soap . . .

"What's going on in the bathroom?" Molly's father called out from the living room. "And why's it taking you so long?"

Later, when she was in bed, Molly put her seal stone under the pillow. And then she heard a very quiet sniffy, snuffly, grunty, growly bark.

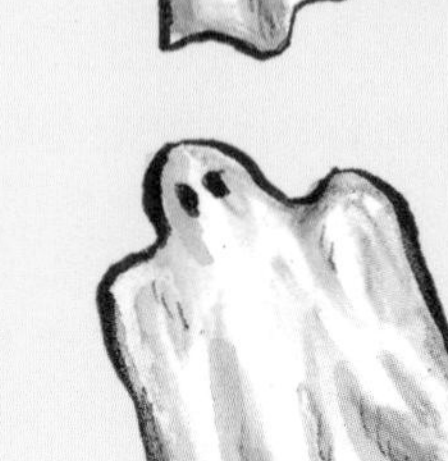

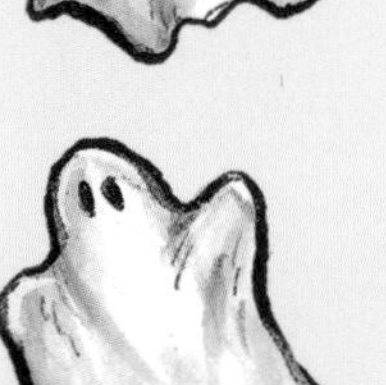

No Biscuits for Ghosts

Molly sat in the big armchair with her legs dangling over the armrest.

"How was school today?" asked her father.

"The teacher told us there's no such thing as ghosts."

Daddy thought about this. "It wasn't always like that. Once upon a time there were lots and lots of ghosts. They were everywhere. They liked it best where

there was complete silence. If someone came and sneezed or a noisy car went roaring by, they'd immediately disappear. Of course they

were always sort of invisible anyway, because most people couldn't see them. Just occasionally they showed themselves, and then they looked more like a puff of air, or a white shadow. And only for a moment or two. But then you'd know there were ghosts around. At night they used to like sitting in little girls' bedrooms. Some of them came just to frighten little girls."

Molly huddled up under her woollen blanket and secretly said to herself, it's true, they do that sometimes. But she didn't say it out loud.

Daddy continued. "Other ghosts came into little girls' bedrooms because they particularly liked little girls and because little girls had lots of nice toys to play with. But things weren't easy for them. People always make a great to-do when they see these strange beings. Ghosts don't like that. Sooner or later they go and look for a quieter place to sleep and disappear for evermore."

Molly suddenly jerked her head around to look at the door. She was pretty sure that something had just flitted round the corner. Or was it just Bertie the cat?

"Anyway, as I said," Daddy went on, "there were lots of ghosts. They sat next to you at the dinner table, hid away in your schoolbag, or hung on the curtain rail. Your Aunt Elsie used to love being with ghosts. Because ghosts, you see, are good company. They don't ask you loads of questions, and they're good listeners. Elsie used to invite a few of these ghostly guests to her house so she wouldn't be all on her own. She'd give them tea and biscuits, but the ghosts never touched them."

That's handy, thought Molly, because then you can eat all the biscuits yourself.

"Most children liked the ghosts. But when the children were jumping around in the playground, the ghosts couldn't join in. On a seesaw, a child is always heavier than a ghost, so it's not much fun if it's all down and no up. And ghosts can't push a swing either. And then there were always people who got angry with them. Because they can really mess things up if they want to. Like making things disappear."

"I know," said Molly knowledgeably. "Especially socks. Mummy is always quite sure she put a pair in the washing machine, but when she puts them on the clothes line, there's only one."

"Exactly," said Daddy. "And eventually people

started blaming ghosts for whatever they didn't like. If there were funny noises outside, they'd say, 'It's a ghost'. Whereas it was just the wind rattling the door. Whenever anything went wrong, they'd say, 'It's those ghosts again'. A lot of people tried to drive the ghosts away, and they thought up all sorts of crazy ways to do it: they lit fires, sang songs, flailed around with their arms or took out all their frustrations on other people. And so the world regulators called a conference. And

they took a vote. The result: a unanimous thumbs down for ghosts. And the fact is, most ghosts did stay away. Nowadays you hardly ever have the good fortune to see one. And even then you have to watch very carefully or you'll miss them. Maybe if you're lucky, you'll see one tonight."

Molly yawned. If Daddy knew that she actually had a ghost friend who watched over her every night in her room, he'd be flabbergasted!

She got up, kissed her father goodnight, and took

herself off to bed. Even though she couldn't see it, she knew that her personal Molly ghost was there and would keep her safe all through the night.

Bird People and Rabbit-Eared Rhinos

Molly and her father were having supper. This evening, as a special treat, there was a dessert: one scoop of vanilla ice cream and one scoop of chocolate ice cream.

Molly did not make a sound apart from the scrape of the spoon and the slurp of the ice cream.

"Mmm, delicious!" sighed Daddy when he'd finished. Then he leaned back in his chair. "How was school today?"

Molly didn't answer straight away. First she had to

eat up the last spoonful, which was half vanilla and half chocolate, half white, half dark. "School was half good and half bad," she said licking her lips and then licking her spoon.

Daddy gave her a quizzical look.

"Maths was boring and general knowledge was fun. The girl on my left was annoying. And the girl on my right was nice. The PE teacher was in a bad mood, and our class teacher was in a good mood."

Daddy pushed his chair back and stood up. "Once upon a time," he said, as they made their way to the living room, "many things were half and half."

Molly took her drawing pad and colouring pencils off the shelf and sat cross-legged on the sofa. "I'm going to draw something that's half house and half tree," she announced.

Daddy had sat down beside her on the sofa and was flicking through the pages of a book. "Once upon a time," he said, "all animals were half and half. Cows were half horse, and horses were half cow."

Molly looked up from her drawing pad with her head leaning to one side. "What did you say?" she asked incredulously.

"In those days there were cowhorses and horsecows," said Daddy cheerfully. "Cowhorses looked like horses at the front and cows at the back. Horsecows were cows at the front, with sporty horsey bottoms at the back."

"But cow legs can't run as fast as horse legs," objected Molly. She jumped down from the sofa and scrambled across the floor on all fours past Bertie, who was curled up in the armchair.

"Look," said Molly. "This is what happens when my arms go faster than my legs." She crawled forwards and almost immediately fell flat on her face. Bertie sat up and watched with great interest. "And when my legs go faster than my arms, this is what happens." Her legs caught up with her stomach, and in no time she was lying on her back. Bertie cocked his head.

"Tell me some more about the mixed animals," she said, returning to the sofa. Daddy shut his book and put his arms behind his head.

"When I was at school," he sighed, "there was a particularly pretty girl in my class, and she had the body of a deer. It was lovely to see, but it meant the girl couldn't do her homework on her own. Because you

can't write if you've only got hooves."

Molly had an idea. "If Bertie could write, he could do my homework for me. He's got nothing else to do all day."

She crawled across to the cat and examined his paws. No, Bertie would never be able to hold a pen in those. And unfortunately there was no sign that he might one day grow some fingers. Molly tore a page out of her drawing pad and began a new picture.

"In those days," her father continued, "there were

also tigers with fish heads. So with their gills they could breathe underwater, but with their legs they could race across the land. They had powerful paws with sharp claws, but they were nowhere near as dangerous as real tigers because they didn't have the teeth. Fish tigers were actually extremely friendly animals, and if you weren't careful, they'd give you a sloppy, slimy, slithery, fishy kiss with their fishy mouths." Daddy puckered up his lips to make a fishy mouth.

"Yuck!" cried Molly, pulling a disgusted face.

"And then there was a rhino that had long rabbit ears. The rabbit-eared rhino had excellent hearing, but

he was very sad most of the time because no one would take him seriously. He'd go rampaging through the countryside, snorting with rage, but people just couldn't stop laughing. Because his long rabbit ears waggled up and down and just looked so ridiculous."

Molly waggled her ears, which she could do extremely well, and tried to imagine what it might be like to have really long rabbit ears. Then she showed her father her new picture. She had drawn a very special sheep. Like normal sheep it stood on four thin legs, but it had a human head.

"A mixture of man and animal – amazing!" said Molly's father. "But look at this. Once upon a time there really were such creatures."

Molly looked at the illustration in the book. It was a stone lion lying in front of a pyramid. And it actually was a lion with a human head.

"Many thousands of years ago," said Daddy, flicking through the book, "there were animals like this in Egypt. And in Ancient Greece they had the minotaur – a man with the head of a bull. If you ever meet one, make sure you cross over to the other side of the street."

Molly was not sure about all this. Normally her father made up his stories, but in this book there were real illustrations of such animal people. So had they actually existed? And could it be that they were still around today? Molly felt a bit uncomfortable. If she did meet a wild man with a bull's head, she certainly would run away as fast as her legs could carry her.

"Fortunately," said her father, "there's no need to be afraid of those creatures any more."

Molly was relieved. But then she thought of another sort of creature. "Mermaids!" she cried. "They're girls with fish tails!"

She bent over her drawing pad. First she drew a girl with long hair and a fish tail instead of legs. Then she drew some blue lines, which were the waves. She put four little scales on the fish tail. They looked like squiggles but they were scales if you said they were scales.

Molly went on drawing and Daddy went on reading. For a while, the only sound was the soft scratching of Molly's coloured pencils and a rustle as Daddy turned a page. Molly licked one of the pencils so that she could colour some seaweed a nice rich green. Then she straightened up. "Why don't they exist any more, all these mixed animal people?" she asked.

Daddy stood up and went to the window. Outside there was a crow strutting across the lawn, cawing as it went. "This is what happened," said Daddy. "Aunt Elsie had a friend. Basically he was a perfectly normal man, except that on his neck he had a bird's head. And in the bird's head there was just one single thought: flying. 'Today is the day,' he would say to Aunt Elsie. 'The sun is shining, the skies are blue – perfect weather for me to

take off into the wide blue yonder.' And out he would go into her garden, flap his arms, race down the garden path at top speed, jump, and land right in the middle of the compost heap. You can just imagine the disappointment – not to mention the smell."

"Funny," murmured Molly. She had remembered Daddy's story about the days when rabbits could fly, but obviously flying rabbits and non-flying birdmen must have happened at different times.

"Something wrong?" asked Daddy.

"No, nothing," said Molly, who now decided that she would also like to fly. She picked up her woollen blanket and put it over her back. Then with arms outstretched she leapt across the living room. But instead of taking off, she got her legs caught in a corner of the blanket, tripped, toppled forward, and just managed to save herself by holding onto the arm of the sofa. She still had

one foot on the blanket though, and it slid forward on the slippery wooden floor. With a despairing wave of her free arm, she fell to the floor and knocked her knee on the leg of the living room table.

"Ooow!" Her father looked on anxiously as the loud cry of pain rang through the room. Slightly dazed, she then sat on the floor rubbing her knee. Tomorrow there would be a big, blue bruise on it. But maybe that wasn't such a bad thing, because she could tell everyone at school that she'd been attacked by a minotaur.

"What happened next?" she asked cheerfully, after her remarkably rapid recovery.

"Aunt Elsie's friend kept doing the same sort of thing as you've just done," Daddy continued. "Eventually, she could no longer bear seeing him so unhappy. 'You've got to get this flying business out of your head,' she urged him. 'If only I could,' whined her friend, 'but all a bird can think about is flying.'

And so in order to comfort him, Aunt Elsie bought two plane tickets and took him with her so that at least once in his life he could say he had flown. But oh dear, oh dear, her friend just sat there sadly looking out of the window with his black bird's eyes. Aunt Elsie could see a teardrop running down the feathers of his face. She felt so sorry for him that as soon as they landed, she telephoned the world regulators. 'My friend needs a new head. To be precise, a human head. Would you please arrange it as quickly as possible.' By now the world regulators had also noticed that the world was a good deal less complicated when everyone had a head that fitted the body. The deer girl, for instance, never really knew whether she was a deer or a girl. And when the fish tiger was on land he always felt something was wrong, but when he was in the water he always felt something wasn't right. He just kept going from one to the other and would really have liked to have a fixed place in the world.

And so the world regulators came to a decision: there should be no more mixed animals. Cows should be cows, and horses should be horses. And that is how Aunt Elsie's friend got a human head. He was even allowed to choose what kind. But whether he should be handsome or ugly, fair-haired or dark-haired, with or without glasses, simply didn't matter two hoots to him.

The only thing he insisted on was a beaky nose, just to remind him of the old days. So if you should happen to meet someone with a beaky nose, it might be Elsie's friend."

Molly thought for a moment and then asked, "If there

are no mixed animals left, what about bats? They have wings and little dogs' heads. And the duckbilled platypus has a beak like a duck and a furry body like a beaver's. Those are mixed animals!"

"You're right as usual," said Daddy with a nod. "When the world regulators did their great big sorting-out operation, the duckbilled platypuses and bats were the ones that got away."

Molly wanted to say something, but she yawned instead.

"Sleepy people should go to bed," said her father.

Molly yawned again. "I'm only half sleepy, though,"

she said. "My arms and legs are sleepy, but my head is still awake."

Then something else occurred to her. "Frank in my class has got a dog with a face like an owl's. But Frank says his dog is a thoroughbred bulldog and is incredibly valuable."

"Hmm," said Daddy. "You can be pretty sure there's still a bit of owl left in the bulldog. And maybe there's a bit of donkey left in Frank."

All of a sudden, Molly no longer felt sleepy. She started to climb onto her father's back.

"I think . . ." But he couldn't say what he was thinking because he now had a mouthful of pyjama sleeve.

"I think," he started again, "my boss at work has the face of a horse."

"And you," said Molly, bending round from behind her father to have a good look at his face, "look like a frog." She let out a croak and dropped down beside him.

Then the sleepiness came again, and she just wanted to stay there on the floor.

"What do I look like?" She crossed her eyes and stuck out her tongue.

"A typical sleepyslug," said Daddy. "You can always recognize a sleepyslug by the fact that it wears pyjamas and can't stop yawning. Sleepyslugs start to act a bit silly when they're up at this hour."

At that moment, Molly's eyes closed.

When she woke up the next morning, she couldn't remember how she had got to bed. Had her father carried her? Had she fallen asleep on the sofa? She could certainly remember the dream she had had. She had

dreamt about a giraffe that was different from normal giraffes. It had a bushy cat's tail, and at the top of its endlessly long neck was Bertie's little cat's face winking at her.

The Dangerous Life of Little People

Molly's legs were dangling over the armrest of the chair.

"So how was school today?" asked her father.

"We all had to stand in a row in order of size, and I was the third tallest girl in my class." Molly was proud of herself. "The teacher said that the biggest people are over two metres tall, and the smallest are the size of small children."

"It wasn't always like that," said her father. Then he pulled a face, sneezed, wiped his nose and walked back and forth in the living room. "Once upon a time there were tiny little people. They were so small that they could stand on a teaspoon. Aunt Elsie had several families of them living on the window sill in the living room. There were a few flowerpots on the sill and the little people lived in tiny houses in the pots, with gardens and everything else they could possibly want. The crumbs of earth looked enormous to them, of course, and what seem like tiny bits of gravel to us were like rocks. You know what I mean?"

How stupid does he think I am? thought Molly, rolled her eyes, and said to her father, "I get it, Daddy. Carry on with the story!"

Her father sneezed again. "You should dry your hair properly after you've been swimming," said Molly with a giggle, "or you'll catch your death of cold." That was what her parents normally said to her.

"The things you say," replied her father, and

continued to pace around the room. "Right, back to the little people. When Aunt Elsie watered the flowers, they put up their tiny little umbrellas. A whole lot of colourful umbrellas – they looked really pretty. But if Aunt Elsie wasn't very careful with the watering, perhaps because

her mind was on something else, it could happen that she poured too much water into the pots. Then their land was flooded. Anyone who couldn't swim had to make sure he got onto a leaf. Then the little people would wave until Aunt Elsie finally arrived and fished them out of the swamp with a slotted spoon. After that they would drip-dry themselves on a kitchen towel. They got pretty fed up with this sort of thing. Of course it was very nice of Aunt Elsie, but they'd have preferred to do without such adventures."

Molly tickled Bertie, who was lying on her lap. Bertie didn't like water at all. "Were there tiny little cats as well?" she asked.

"Of course," said Daddy. "They were so tiny that they could fit onto your fingernail. Very sweet." But difficult to stroke, thought Molly, as she blew into Bertie's ear. Bertie was not amused.

"For a long time the big people and the little people got on well together," Daddy continued. "They shared the housework: the little ones took care of the places the big ones couldn't get to. The corners behind radiators, for instance, and the nooks and crannies in different rooms. They drove up in their tiny fork-lift trucks and lorries, constructed tiny scaffolding up the walls, and made tiny repairs and tiny brushstrokes. And they drank huge quantities of beer out of their tiny bottles."

Molly giggled quietly and drank a giant mouthful of apple juice out of her giant glass.

"The big people," continued Daddy, "made sure that the little people had a nice spot in their homes – in the kitchen cupboard, or in a shoe box, or on a bookshelf. Above all, the place had to be safe, because the big people's pets were a real problem. Aunt Elsie, for example, had a tabby cat. He was always lurking around

and would have liked nothing better than to hunt the little people."

Molly had once seen Bertie playing with a mouse. She shuddered at the thought of it being one of the little people. But at the moment, Bertie was lying lazily on her lap. He didn't look at all dangerous. He just looked cuddly.

"The little people were happiest when there were little children with dolls' houses," said Daddy. "One like yours, with a bedroom, living room, dining room, bathroom and kitchen. And proper little furniture. Aunt Elsie also had a doll's house. The Popply family lived in it – father, mother and three little Popplies. Sometimes the five Popplies went to see the Pimplies, who lived in the flowerpot. Then they all had supper together. One potato was enough for all of them, and their mini dog Wuffy also had a piece. Afterwards, they would sit round a candle stump and tell one another stories. Most

of the stories were moans about the big people and how inconsiderate they were.

And one day it reached the point where they'd all had enough. The little people wanted to be big. Their lives had become much more dangerous, and they complained that they were always dependent on the big people, which simply wasn't fair. The Pimplies staged a demonstration and marched up and down Aunt Elsie's

window sill holding tiny banners and shouting, 'equal size for all, equal size for all . . .' More and more little people joined the protest march on the window sill. Then they went on strike, and at night they climbed onto the big people's pillows and shouted in their ears: 'equal size for all, equal size for all!' Eventually the big people had had enough. Something had to be done.

And so the world regulators called another conference. While they were discussing what to do, the telephone rang. Aunt Elsie was on the line. 'Give them what they're asking for!' she shouted. 'Make them big if big is what they want to be!' She was furious, because the Pimply family had now started sawing off the leaves of all her pot plants. The world regulators didn't much like having Aunt Elsie yelling at them, and so they quickly

reached a decision. They decreed that all people should be of equal size. Except for basketball players, who are always bigger than everyone else so that they can plonk the ball in the basket."

While her father had been talking, Molly had been eating an apple. Now she held the core in the palm of her hand and imagined that it was a tiny girl in a blue

dress with long black hair and teeny weeny brown shoes. Maybe, she thought to herself, a girl like that might come and tell me stories about the world of the little people before I go to sleep. "I'm off to bed," she said to her father.

"Eh, what? That's very sudden," said her father in surprise, though he wasn't really at all surprised because Molly was always surprising him.

Very carefully, Molly carried the apple core into her room. And very carefully she laid it next to her on the pillow and covered it with her handkerchief so that only its head peeped out. But before the girl in the blue dress with the long black hair and the brown shoes could tell her a single story, Molly was fast asleep. She dreamed about a whole classroom full of little people, who slipped

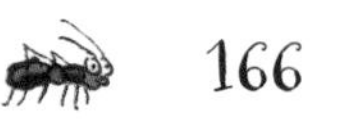

into her bed with their tiny covers, and then picked up their tiny pillows and had an enormous pillow fight.

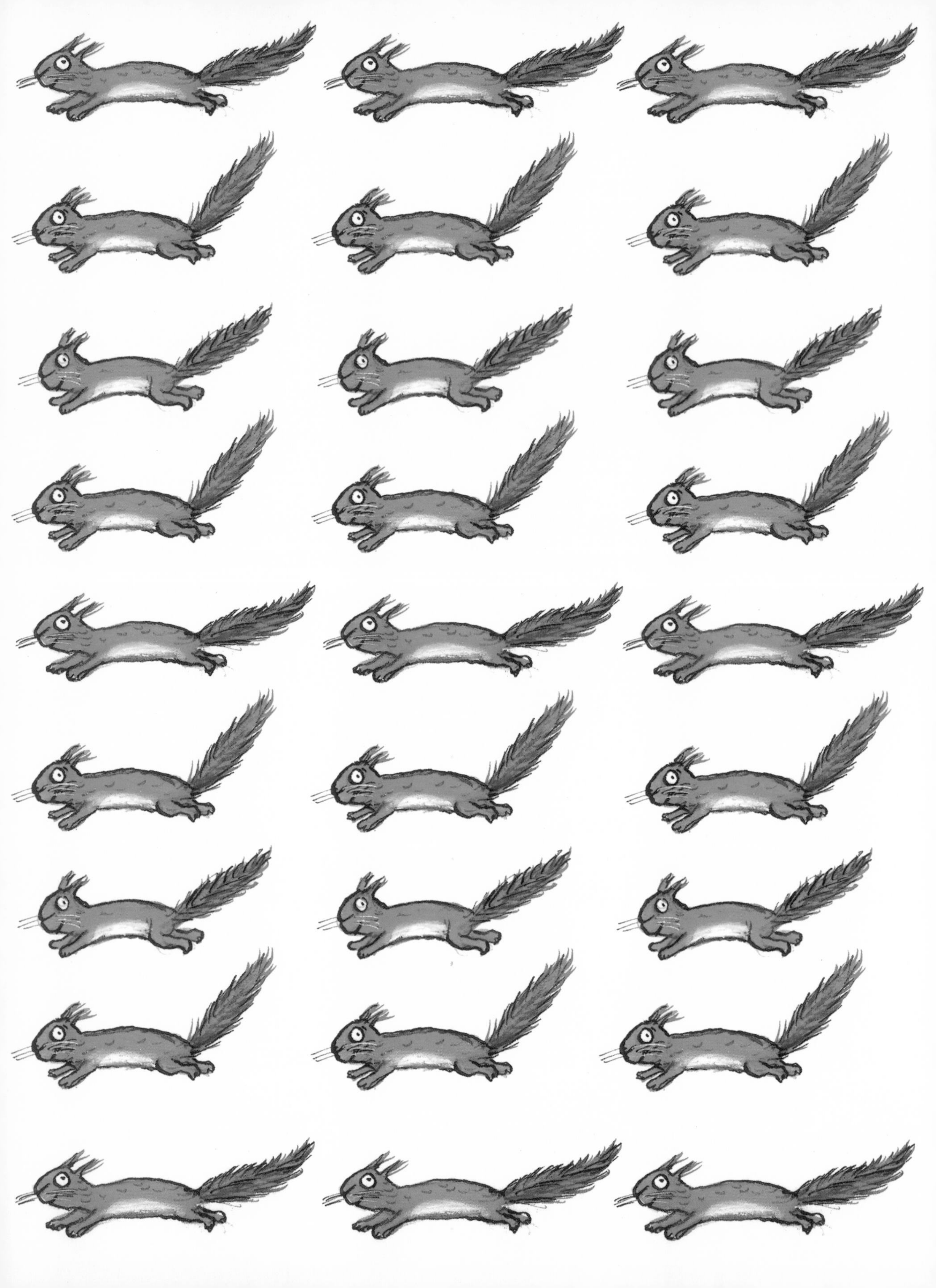

Singing Squirrels and Talking Dogs

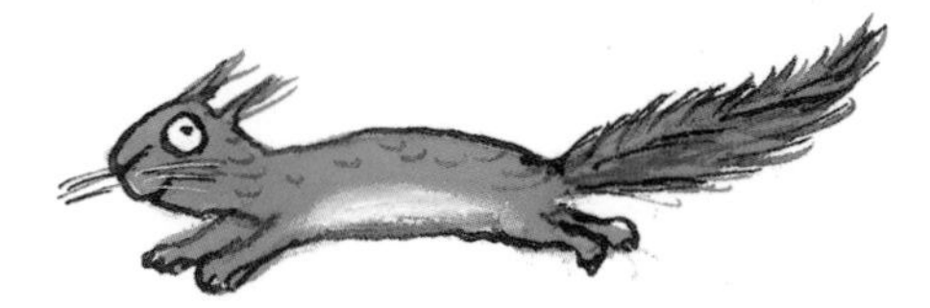

"Look out, I'm coming!" yelled Molly as she took a run-up and made a giant leap onto the sofa. She landed right next to her father, who dropped his newspaper out of sheer shock.

"Can you make it a bit gentler next time, please," grumbled Daddy, as he folded up his newspaper and leaned back on the sofa. "How was school today?"

Molly didn't answer straight away. She hadn't been to school. Daddy had forgotten that there was no school

today. And he'd forgotten that he'd dropped Molly off at her friend Henry's house that morning. She had spent the whole day at Henry's. I'd better think of something, though, she thought to herself, or otherwise there won't be any stories today. And then she had an idea. Henry had told her that his budgerigar was a great talker. But it turned out that all the budgie could say was 'hello' and 'budgie'.

Molly turned to her father. "The teacher told us that

humans are the only beings in the world that can talk."

Molly had hit the spot, because her father at once embarked on a new story. "It wasn't always like that," he said. He cleared his throat, rose to his feet, walked up and down, and then sat in his armchair so that he could look out into the garden.

"Once upon a time, animals talked just like us humans. Loud and clear."

"What did their voices sound like?" asked Molly.

Her father made a few funny noises – first a deep grunt, then a not-so-deep croak, and then a high-pitched cheep. Those were supposed to be animal voices. They didn't sound very convincing, and they certainly didn't sound very nice.

"So they weren't nice voices?" said Molly tentatively, looking sideways at her father.

"Oh yes, some of them had

absolutely beautiful voices," replied her father, slightly offended. "Some animals had fantastic singing voices – and not just the birds. Squirrels, for example. Aunt Elsie used to have a squirrel choir in her garden. They rehearsed every Tuesday. At three o'clock sharp they'd come hopping out of the forest, each squirrel carrying a nut under one arm for a little nibble during the break."

Molly took a few pretzel sticks from the table and imagined being a squirrel choir girl during rehearsal break.

"Did they have a conductor?"

"Of course. The mole was the conductor."

"He couldn't have been!" cried Molly. "Moles live underground. They can't stand the light!"

"Ha, that's what sunglasses are for," said Daddy. "When he was conducting, the mole obviously wore sunglasses."

Molly jumped up and began to conduct a choir. She closed her eyes as she did so, because she knew that moles are more or less blind. Bertie the cat immediately sensed the danger and went and hid under the sofa.

"So what did they sing, the squirrels?" Molly asked as she went hopping round her father.

"Love songs, pop songs – squirrel pop of course. Very modern."

"Sing one!" pleaded Molly. "Please, Daddy!"

Her father pursed his lips and in a high squeaky voice sang: "Squirrel-di-dee, squirrel-di-doo, Cyril my squirrel, I'm nuts about you."

Molly laughed. Her father was hopeless at singing.

"Aunt Elsie was a real fan of the squirrels," Daddy continued. "Every Tuesday she sat out on the patio tapping her foot to the beat. And when the rehearsal was over, she invited the squirrels to join her at the garden table. She gave them little bowls of peanuts. And then they would have a chat about this and that."

Molly had got tired of jumping around, so she sat down on the sofa. "All Aunt Elsie ever talks about is recipes and her hairstyle. Were the squirrels interested?"

"Not really," admitted her father. "No, I can't say they were. They just listened out of politeness because Aunt Elsie was so nice to them. They'd have preferred to talk about where you can find nuts in winter, or how to build the warmest possible nest. Unfortunately Aunt Elsie didn't have a clue about such things. When the conversation turned to nut cake, they did prick up their ears, but it wasn't long before they went to sleep out of boredom and fell off their chairs. That was a bit frustrating for poor Aunt Elsie, because she couldn't hold much of a conversation with her dog either."

"Her dog?" Molly asked incredulously. Aunt Elsie

had never had a dog in her life, because she couldn't stand dogs. But Molly didn't want to interrupt her father.

"Oh yes, Aunt Elsie had a dog. His name was Conrad and he could tell great jokes. He was the best dog joke-teller in the world. All the animals used to laugh themselves silly. But only animals. Not people, because people didn't get the jokes. In fact, Conrad's jokes made Aunt Elsie squirm. Because they were rather rude.

And since humans never laughed at them, animals only told them when they were among themselves."

Molly thought of the cows in the meadow which she passed on her way to school. Maybe the cows told one another jokes as well while they munched the grass all day long. Tomorrow she would stop at the field and listen in.

"And since humans kept on talking about all this useless stuff," Daddy continued, "one day the animals decided it was stupid to carry on. So they called an animal world regulator conference. The Chairman – an old rabbit who had turned completely grey – hopped onto the compost heap and delivered a speech. 'Humans do not get our jokes. They constantly talk about things that are of no interest whatsoever to us. Cars,

babies' nappies, computers, fashion, recipes, hairdressers' appointments – it's all deadly boring. And so we need to make up our own language. Then no squirrel will ever again fall off their chair out of sheer boredom.' All the animals applauded. And so that is why animals now speak their own language, and we humans can no longer understand what they're saying."

Daddy had ended his story and drank a mouthful of tea from his cup. Molly thought about what he had told her. What he didn't know was that she did understand animal language. Or at least she understood Bertie's language. He rubbed up against her legs, and Molly knew exactly what he was saying to her: "It's time for little girls and little cats to go to bed." And every morning, when he rubbed up against her legs, again she knew exactly what he wanted. It meant: "I'm hungry."

Molly gave her father a goodnight kiss and had a last look out of the window at the garden. The two squirrels that had been playing in the tree outside the window had gone now. If there had been rabbits in the garden instead, thought Molly, Daddy would have told her about a rabbit choir.

She had just snuggled up under the covers when a fly started buzzing round her nose.

"Go away!" said Molly.

"No," said the fly. "Why should I?"

"Because you're stopping me from sleeping. Go away!"

"No," said the fly, and buzzed around again. "It's fun dancing on your nose."

"You are going to fly away NOW," said Molly.

"No I'm not," said the fly.

"Yes you are," said Molly.

The conversation continued to flow this way and that until Molly fell asleep – in spite of the fly. He flew back to his friends and with great excitement reported that he'd just been talking to a human. He hadn't done that for a very, very long time.

When Daddy Changed Into a Donkey

Daddy was sitting in his armchair reading the paper. "Molly!" he shouted. No answer. "Where are you?"

Then he heard a quiet swishing, rustling sound. The door opened, and in came Molly. But she was hardly recognizable.

"Who are you, madam?" asked Daddy. "I don't think we've ever had the pleasure of being introduced."

Molly was in disguise. On her nose sat a pair of sunglasses, and over her pyjamas she was wearing a red silk dress. Both belonged to her mother. The thin material flapped round Molly's little body. Her hands had disappeared under the sleeves, which were far too long, and she had to hold the hem up with one hand so that it didn't sweep the floor.

Daddy sucked the air between his teeth. "Lucky Mummy's not here to see this," he murmured. He looked down anxiously at the high-heeled shoes which were clearly bending as Molly teetered across the room on them – cautiously, step by step, because she could hardly see a thing through the sunglasses. Bertie the cat took the precaution of hiding away under the sofa.

"Guess who I am!" cried Molly, turning around in a circle.

"Another princess?"

Molly shook her head. "I'm a famous film star." She carefully perched on the edge of the sofa. "And

you're my butler. Butler, I'd like an apple juice and some pretzel sticks."

Daddy got up with a sigh. A moment later he came back with a two glasses of apple juice, and a packet of pretzel sticks. "Wait," he said, as he laid everything out on the table. "I'd also like to be somebody else."

Molly nibbled a pretzel stick and listened to the crunching sound in her head. It mingled with a cheerful whistling from the bedroom. "Daddy?" she called out.

"Coming!" answered an unfamiliar voice. And there in the doorway stood her father. Molly burst out laughing. He had tied a flowery scarf round his head and had put on a long blue summer skirt over his trousers.

"Those are Mummy's things too!" cried Molly. She couldn't help laughing again, because her father looked so funny. He had also put on a pair of glasses – the black plastic ones that Molly had worn at the funfair last year.

And attached to the glasses was a great big nose with a horrible wart on it.

"I am Grandma Greta Grampian," croaked Daddy, disguising his voice. Bent double, he shuffled across to the sofa, and he really looked like a very frail old woman. "My home is a hut in the forest, and day and night there is thick smoke coming out of the chimney, because day in and day out I brew secret magic potions on my stove. I am about a hundred and twenty years old, but nobody knows for sure."

"But you've only changed your clothes," said Molly. "You aren't really an old woman. If I could really be a famous film star, wouldn't that be great!" She liked her next idea even more. "Or I could be someone living in the jungle. Then I could have breakfast with the monkeys every morning."

Molly could just see herself eating muesli with a family of chimpanzees, and what a mess they would make of the breakfast table. There would be one dipping his long fingers in the jar of marmalade, and the others spilling their coffee all over the place. But then she realized that there probably wouldn't be any milk or muesli in the jungle. She shrugged her shoulders. "Unfortunately that's just impossible because you can never be somebody else."

"It wasn't always like that," said Daddy. "But first, would you please . . ."

Molly knew what he was going to say. She took off the dress – it was uncomfortable anyway – grabbed hold of her woollen blanket and snuggled up next to her father.

"Once upon a time, you could choose who or what you wanted to be," he began, chasing away a fly that had just lost its way and landed on his nose. "You could change into someone different every day."

"Could I have been an Apache warrior then?" Molly could picture herself with black hair fluttering in the wind as she galloped over the prairie on her black and white pony.

"Of course," said Daddy, "you could be whatever you felt like being."

"Even a mail van, or a beetle?"

"Nothing simpler. A fly. The Pope."

"Or a show jumper," added Molly thoughtfully. "What would you have wanted to change into?" she asked, peeping up at him. If only he knew how daft he looked in those silly glasses!

Daddy stood up and looked out of the window at the back garden. "In the old days I liked to turn myself into a donkey in the mornings, so that I didn't have to go to work. I spent the whole day standing in the field in the sunshine, and did nothing but eat and relax. Ah, those were the good old days!" He stretched his arms and let out a sigh.

It wasn't hard for Molly to imagine her father as a donkey out in a field. Even as a human being he sometimes just stood around for hours in the garden looking at trees and flowers and never getting at all bored. "So who did your work in the office?" she asked.

"A donkey," he answered promptly. "We simply

swapped. The donkey turned into me, and went to the office in my place."

Molly looked at him incredulously. "But didn't anyone notice?"

"Yes, once the donkey almost gave the game away. It was in a meeting, and by mistake he let out a loud 'heehaw!' 'Would you please express yourself a little more clearly,' said the boss. And the others whispered among themselves: 'Oh dear, our colleague doesn't seem to be quite himself today.'"

Molly giggled.

"After that incident, I thought it was better to pick a penguin to take my place. He looked just right for office work in his black suit, and fitted in perfectly with all the other suit-wearers. He was very hardworking too, the penguin. And I had a good time just lazing around." Once again he sighed. "I only remained myself at the weekend."

Molly had a big decision to make. What would she most like to change herself into? She had a great idea. She would be somebody different on each day of the week.

"Listen, Daddy. On Mondays I'd change myself into

our neighbour. Then I could walk his dog all day. On Tuesdays I'd work in a bakery, so I could eat as much cake as I like. And on Wednesdays . . ." Molly closed her eyes and had a little think. "On Wednesdays I'd like to be a bird, then I could see our house from above. On Thursdays I'd be a fish in the sea and swim once round the world. On Fridays . . ."

"On Fridays you could be Queen of England," said her father. "Then you could pass a law saying no school on Fridays."

Molly nodded. That was not a bad idea. But if she was Queen of England, she would probably get rid of school altogether. And that girl opposite, who always got on her nerves – she'd get rid of her too. Molly tried to do a handstand, but as that was too difficult on the soft cushions of the sofa, she changed it into a somersault.

"At weekends, I'd stay as Molly. Otherwise you'd never find me."

Daddy looked round the living room. "Then I'd think my daughter might have changed into a reading lamp – she sometimes has such crazy ideas. And so I'd tell stories to the reading lamp. And the lamp would think: That man's crazy – he thinks I'm his daughter and I'm just a reading lamp."

In the meantime, Molly had put all the sofa cushions on top of one another and was now enthroned up on the pile. She asked, "Why can't we change ourselves any more?" and she thought to herself that it was bound to be because of Aunt Elsie.

"It's because of Aunt Elsie," said Daddy. He was still wearing the skirt, scarf and sunglasses. A few passers-by were standing outside on the pavement at the front of the house, looking into the living room. Molly thought her father's outfit was a little embarrassing, but she

waved cheerfully to them. The people went on their way, shaking their heads.

"This is what happened," her father continued, oblivious to the spectators. "Aunt Elsie had a little house with a beautiful garden. In it grew sunflowers as tall as the house, the finest roses for miles around, and dazzling exotic plants that you couldn't find anywhere else. There were a few fountains softly splashing away, and hundreds of butterflies flying around. It wasn't long before news of this attraction spread. Tourists came from here, there and everywhere to see the famous garden. Aunt Elsie was flattered, and was happy to open her garden gate to all and sundry."

Molly saw the expression on her father's face suddenly darken. He was gazing at the flowerbed outside the window. A shining red dahlia was lying broken on the ground.

"Then more and more tourists came, whole busloads

of them," he went on, visibly upset. "They trampled all over Aunt Elsie's primroses and her forget-me-nots and all her fantastic exotic plants and even her favourite dahlias. That was upsetting. Very, very upsetting!"

Molly had a bad conscience about the broken dahlia. All she'd wanted to do was have a little game of football. She hid her face behind a cushion, and to take her father's mind off the dahlia, she quickly asked him, "So what did Aunt Elsie do?"

Her father pushed the scarf to one side so that he could scratch his ear. "Aunt Elsie finally lost patience. 'That's enough!' she howled. 'Get out, all of you!' The people left the garden, grumbling like mad. Just one of them didn't leave. He was absolutely determined to carry on walking through the garden. And as everybody could turn into anybody in those days, this man came up with a special trick: he changed himself into Aunt Elsie. That meant he could wander round the garden all

day long without being recognized. Until he happened to bump into the real Aunt Elsie. So there stood the real Elsie suddenly confronted by a woman who looked exactly the same as her." Daddy paused for a moment to give Molly time to think about it.

That's what it must be like if you look in the mirror and your reflection suddenly comes to life, thought Molly. She liked the idea.

"A twin sister!" she cried. "Was Aunt Elsie pleased?"

Daddy shook his head. "On the contrary. It gave Aunt Elsie a terrible shock. 'Who are you?' she cried. 'I'm Elsie,' replied the other woman. 'You can't be,' yelled Aunt Elsie indignantly. 'I happen to know that without a shadow of a doubt, I am me!' And so the argument went back and forth. And then it all turned even nastier."

Daddy took a deep breath. "Other

people had been standing by the garden fence, and they overheard the quarrel. Good idea, they thought, and so they played the same transformation trick. Just half an hour later, the garden was full of Elsies."

Molly clapped her hands in front of her face. "Wowee!" she gasped, shaking with laughter.

"The sight of all these Elsies made the squirrels feel

dizzy," said Daddy. "The birds were so shocked that they fell down from the trees. And the butterflies all went out of their tiny butterfly minds. Because when they flew from flower to flower, there was an Aunt Elsie standing beside each one. And all the Elsies smelt of the same perfume. The butterflies fluttered round in circles, totally confused. You can just imagine the uproar."

Daddy sat down next to Molly on the sofa. "And so once again Aunt Elsie rang the world regulators, and very calmly she said to them, 'Would you please come and see the chaos here?' The world regulators jumped into the nearest taxi and came racing to the garden. But they didn't know which Elsie to speak to. Hundreds of women, all looking identical, were all yelling at the same time, 'I'm Elsie!' 'No, I am!'"

Molly grabbed hold of her father's arm, and put her other hand over his mouth because she wanted to tell

the rest of the story herself. "The world regulators said, 'Things can't go on like this'. And so they put a ban on everybody changing themselves into anybody." Molly let go of her father.

"That's exactly what happened," he said, pulling the scarf off his head. "Which in fact was a pity. Because otherwise I could turn myself into an inventor now. And then I would invent a robot which would clear the dishes and tidy the kitchen."

Bertie jumped up onto the sofa. Molly immediately set about trying to transform him into a wild and dangerous monster with the aid of the woollen blanket. She lifted him and the blanket as high as she could, and pretended they were sailing through the air. Bertie became a flying dragon with gigantic claws. His little mouth changed into dark, cavernous jaws with flames shooting out of them. Bertie mewed, and Molly let him down. He jerked himself free and raced away.

"How about you giving me a hand in the kitchen?" asked her father.

Molly was happy to do so, but first she had to tickle her father. And she tickled him so hard that he let out a noise that sounded rather like Bertie's miaow.

"I'd really like best of all to be a princess," said Molly a little later, while they were putting the plates in the dishwasher.

Daddy frowned. "I'd think very carefully about that," he said. "Being a princess is a rotten job. Princesses have to get up at five o'clock every morning, read ten newspapers, and then hold one audience after another. They have to sit on their hard gold throne hour after hour, listening to other people's problems. In any case, there's nothing really special about princesses."

Molly had to agree. Most of the girls in her class would change themselves into princesses like a shot if

they were able to. A whole class of princesses? Molly pulled a face.

"The question is: would you actually like to be someone else?" asked her father. "Because if you were, you wouldn't have Mummy, or me, or Bertie."

There was no need for him to say more. Molly had already made up her mind. She wanted to remain Molly – at least for tonight.

Later, when she was in the bathroom, she looked in the mirror. "No need for you to look at me like that," she said to the face that was looking back at her. "I'm Molly. You're just my reflection." The reflection didn't answer. But the fact that it wanted to be Molly was crystal clear, because whatever faces Molly pulled, the reflection copied exactly.

Molly slid into bed, and her father kissed her goodnight. During the night, she suddenly woke up when Bertie jumped into bed with her. He had been

mouse-hunting in the garden, and had heroically driven off the fat cat that belonged to the neighbours. Now he cuddled up close to Molly, laying his head on his white paws. After that, Molly slept like a stone, but Bertie dreamed that he was a tiger, bigger and stronger than every other animal in the jungle. Because there could only be one ruler of the jungle, and that was Bertie, the Tiger King.

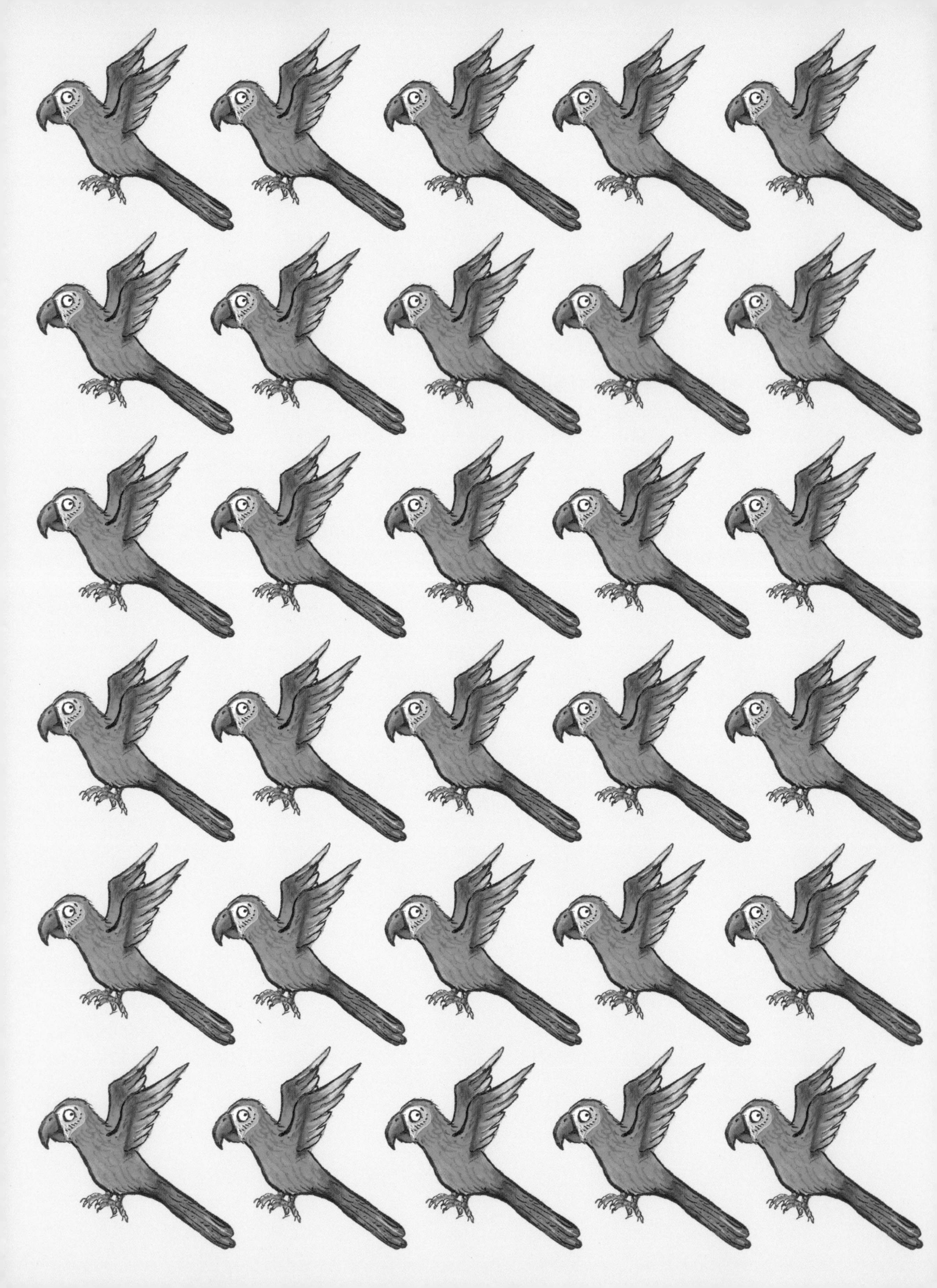

Wild Pets

When Daddy came home from shopping, he couldn't find Molly anywhere. The woollen blanket was draped over the dining table and fixed to the arms of the chairs with clothes pegs. On top of the blanket lay Bertie, his four legs stretched out in all directions.

"Where's Molly?" asked her father. "Has she perhaps left home?" A quiet squeaking and squealing came from the hollow space under the blanket. "What's this? Have we got pigs in here?" he wondered, wide-eyed.

The woollen blanket squeak-squealed again, this time loud and clear.

"Strange," said Daddy, making himself comfortable on the sofa. "Pigs live in a pigsty." And then he said, "But it wasn't always like that."

Everything went quiet under the woollen blanket.

"Once upon a time, lots of different animals lived in people's houses, even fat woolly bears, because they realized that they could make a superb bear cave out of a woollen blanket, a table and a few chairs."

A low rumble came from the blanket cave.

Daddy stretched out on the sofa, put a cushion under his head, and looked up at the ceiling. "Monkeys had discovered what fun it was swinging around on the lights in the ceiling. From there they could jump onto the curtain rails, then to the cupboard, and finally to their favourite place of all, the bookcase. They took out every book one by one, and threw them as far as

they could. Monkeys called that 'tidying up'."

The woollen blanket giggled. This was followed by a noise like someone biting an apple.

"But who am I telling this to? Molly isn't here!"

"Yes I am!" cried Molly, and an arm poked out from under the blanket. In its hand was a half-eaten apple.

"Ugh!" said Daddy. "That's just an arm with an apple in it. Any old arm could come along and say, 'I'm Molly.'"

There was a rustling sound and a bare foot poked out. "And now?" asked the voice of the woollen blanket.

"Hmm. This foot reminds me that we had to buy some new shoes recently, because Molly's feet have grown again."

"Exactly," said the woollen blanket. "Green shoes with red laces."

"These feet are really enormous," said Daddy in surprise. "Almost as big as kangaroo feet. Incidentally, kangaroos also used to live with people, because they enjoyed jumping over woollen blanket bear caves."

"What about lions?" asked the blanket.

"Hmm," mused Daddy. "When a lion isn't eating, what he likes best is sleeping. And where can you find a softer place to sleep than a human bed?"

"If he makes himself nice and small," said the blanket, "the lion can sleep with Bertie and me in my bed. But only if he doesn't eat Bertie."

"We'll make sure the lion is always full," said Daddy. "Then he'll certainly leave Bertie alone. In fact, maybe he'll find Bertie so adorable that he'll adopt him, and then Bertie can go and live with the lion cubs in the lion family."

"What about elephants?" asked the blanket.

"Hmm," said Daddy again, and he sighed. "Where there are lions, there are also elephants. I think that's because they're good friends. Or they all belong to the same tennis club."

The blanket giggled again and said, "But elephants are ginormous. There's no way they can move around in human houses. They wouldn't even be able to get through the door. Did the elephants just stand around doing nothing?"

"Certainly not," replied her father. "Aunt Elsie's elephant for one was very hardworking. He was a shower elephant."

"A what?" asked the blanket.

"A shower elephant is an elephant that stands in the

bathroom and works as a shower. That's why he's got a trunk."

Daddy stood up and then bent down towards the woollen blanket cave. "Any room in there?"

"No-o-o!" cried Molly, poking her head out for just a fraction of a second.

Daddy fished around for a cushion and then lay down on the floor next to the cave. With one finger he raised a corner of the woollen blanket.

"Just the head?" he pleaded.

"Oh, all right," said Molly generously.

She moved a little in order to make room. Now that her father's head was right next to hers, his voice sounded quite different and was louder.

"Were there other animals in the house?" she whispered.

"Just a parrot and a whole lot of ants," answered Daddy. "There was no room for any more. Because in the evening they all wanted to sit on the sofa and watch TV. From the very start the kangaroo made sure he got the best seat, right in the middle, while the others were still eating or doing their homework. Left and right of the kangaroo sat the elephant and the bear, and the pig and lion squeezed in at the two ends. The kangaroo was all squashed up."

"And why aren't the animals there any more?" asked Molly.

"They emigrated," answered Daddy. "'It's too cramped in here,' they announced one day, 'so we're going to emigrate.' 'I'll go to Africa,' roared the lion, and of course the elephant said he'd go with him. The monkey and the parrot said the same. 'I'm going to Australia, and then I'll be rid of you lot,' said the kangaroo. 'Africa, Australia – both much too hot for me,' rumbled the bear. 'I'm going to Alaska.' Only the ants stayed here. But at some time even they moved out into the garden, because they had quite a few problems with Aunt Elsie."

A tiny gust of wind blew under the woollen blanket. Molly heard the front door close and Bertie leaping down off the table.

"Anyone at home? Hi, Bertie!"

It was Mummy's voice. Molly put her fingers over Daddy's lips. They heard Mummy enter the room.

"That's strange," they heard her say. "I can only see

a body with arms and legs. They might all belong to my husband. But just a few days ago my husband, if I remember rightly, also had a head. So it can't be him.

Even though it was dark down in the cave, Molly could see tiny worry lines forming on her father's face. She stuck an arm out from under the blanket.

"Oooh!" said Mummy in surprise. "There's an arm, and it doesn't fit in with the other body at all. It looks more like my daughter's, but I can't see her anywhere either. Maybe I picked the wrong front door. Maybe this isn't my house! I think I'd better leave." Her footsteps started going away.

"Stoooppp!" cried Molly, and she crawled out of the cave and jumped into her mother's arms.

That evening, bedtime came later than usual, because Molly and her mother had so much to talk about. Before she went to sleep, Molly put all her stuffed toys on the bedhead behind her. She wanted them to be

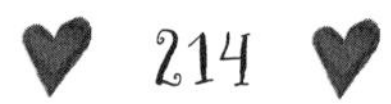

comfortable so that none of them would suddenly think of emigrating.

Molly fell into a deep sleep. So deep that she had no dreams at all during the night. And so deep that she didn't even know that her mother came in, sat down beside her on the bed, and stayed there for quite a while, looking at her as she slept.